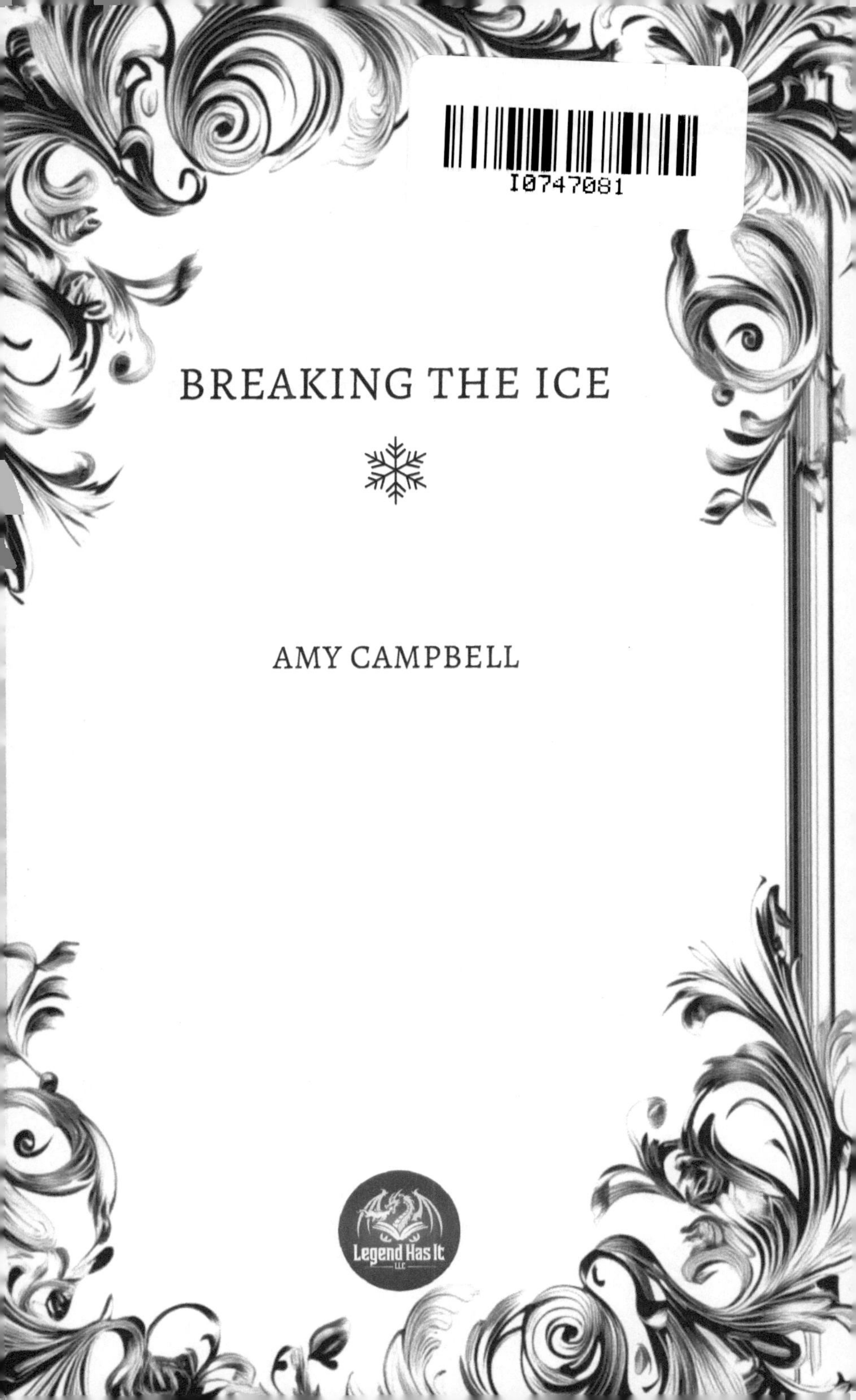

BREAKING THE ICE

AMY CAMPBELL

For those who fight for what's right, even when it's hard. Even when it's the darkest of times.

Cover design by Amy Campbell
First edition: November 2025
www.amycampbell.info

v 101625

AUTHOR'S NOTE

Breaking the Ice is a story of rebellion and resilience, but such journeys are rarely simple or painless. Some parts of the story may be challenging for readers. Please be aware that *Breaking the Ice* includes depictions of emotional and verbal abuse, enslavement and exploitation, implied sexual exploitation, toxic family dynamics, manipulation and coercion, violence, and imprisonment.

CHAPTER 1

Power didn't whisper in the Wells ballroom—it roared, draped in silk and drowning in champagne. The crystal chandeliers above cast a fractured, dazzling light across the room, their brilliance bending and refracting off glasses of bubbly and the glittering jewelry of Ganland's elite. The Wells estate had become the epicenter of opulence tonight, a palace of decadence where smiles masked cruelty and laughter drowned out murmurs of corruption.

Malcolm Wells stood near the edge of it all, a silent observer in the shadow of his father's magnetic presence. At just eighteen, he was not only old enough to play the part expected of him, but also of an age to feel the overwhelming burden of it. Stafford Wells held court at the center of the room, his booming laugh shattering the hum of conversation like a cannonball. Malcolm's hand tightened around his untouched glass of wine, the cool condensation seeping into his palm.

Malcolm's black coat, trimmed with silver embroidery, fit him like a second skin. At the moment, he felt much like a snake and was prepared to shed that skin. The fabric itched where it brushed his neck, each thread a prickling reminder of his status.

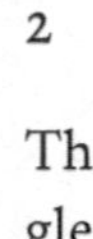

The Wells family crest, a coiled serpent with rubies for eyes, gleamed on the collar—a reminder of what he was. Of who he was meant to be.

Around him, the room thrummed with false cheer. A string quartet played a lively tune, the kind meant to evoke the spirit of Midwinter, but to Malcolm it sounded hollow. The celebration had only just begun, the first of many gatherings in a month-long season of revelry and excess. Outside the frosted windows, an unseasonable chill gripped the world, the wind rattling the glass and setting the lanterns strung along the estate's grand drive swaying. Inside, however, the warmth was stifling, the air thick with the heady scents of pine boughs, spiced wine, and the rich tang of perfume.

"Smile, Malcolm," Stafford rumbled as he sidled up to him, his lips curved into the charming grin he reserved for the crowd. His breath smelled faintly of brandy, and the scent curled around the words like smoke. "You look like you're attending a funeral, not a holiday gala."

Malcolm forced a smile, slipping on the mask he always wore around his father. The muscles in his face ached from the effort, but he met Stafford's gaze with the practiced blankness of someone who had long since mastered the art of self-erasure. Stafford's grin widened, but the warmth in it was as false as the cheer in the room.

"That's better," his father murmured, his tone cutting beneath the veneer of approval. "Try not to embarrass me tonight, son. The Duncans are here, and Everett's been asking about your plans to expand operations in the northern territories. You'll make yourself useful and assuage his concerns, won't you?"

The words were a command, not a question. Malcolm nodded mutely, his jaw tightening as Stafford's hand rested on his shoulder a moment longer than necessary—a gesture of dominance, not affection. Then Stafford was gone, swept back

into the throng of glittering guests, his laughter ringing out as he moved from one conversation to the next.

Stafford Wells was correct about one thing: it was the Midwinter holiday, a time for celebration. Once, Malcolm had loved the season. As a boy, he had reveled in the traditions—the exchange of gifts, the glow of hearth fires, the decadent sweets that seemed to appear on every surface. Now, the holiday felt empty, its joy smothered under the realities of life. Malcolm turned toward the bar, deciding that the best course of action might be to drown his sorrows in something stronger than nostalgia.

And that was when he saw her.

She stood near the far end of the room, half-hidden in the shadow of the towering evergreen. The tree's ornaments reflected pinpricks of light onto her face, a soft glow that seemed to set her apart from the crowd. Her bright pink hair— an unusual, striking color—caught the light like spun sugar. Unlike the other women circulating through the room like butterflies, she wore a simple gown. The plain black fabric marked her as one of the house staff. A neatly pressed apron tied around her waist further cemented her station. She balanced a tray with wine glasses in one hand and a bottle in the other, navigating her way through the revelers as if they were a pack of wolves ready to pounce on her at any moment.

Flora, his mind supplied. He'd seen her name on the manifest of new acquisitions that had arrived from the processing center just two weeks ago, written in neat, impersonal script. Half-knocker heritage, it had noted, which accounted for her colorful hair. From his vantage point, she looked like a diminutive human, but he knew if he moved closer, he'd see the telltale grey undertones of her stone-like skin—the mark of her knocker parent. The manifest had described her features clinically, reducing her to a list of traits: height, build, age, and *exotic appeal*.

Malcolm's jaw clenched as he hissed out a slow breath, a bitter taste rising in his throat. She was a commodity. That was the mindset he was expected to adopt, the one drilled into him from the moment he could read those damn manifests. But it turned his stomach now, that cold, dispassionate view. Flora wasn't an artifact to be cataloged or a rare gem to be displayed —she was a person. And yet, here she was, standing in the lion's den, her gaze sweeping the room with an expression that bordered on contempt. It was the look of someone who understood the game but refused to play by its rules.

Malcolm also knew, according to the manifest, the future in store for the mystic woman. Her unusual looks would make her a popular bed companion among the elites, a fate as vile as it was inevitable. She deserved better. Deserved freedom. But standing here, trapped in his father's world, he couldn't stand against it.

Before he could dwell further, a sugary voice interrupted his thoughts, and he turned to see Cinna, her painted lips curved into a promising smile. Cinna's gown shimmered like liquid gold, clinging to her curves in a way that demanded attention, and her hair, a cascade of glossy curls, had been arranged just so, framing her face like a portrait on display. Every detail of her appearance had been curated for maximum effect.

"I was beginning to think you'd forgotten me," she said, her tone a perfect balance of teasing and reproach.

Her fingers skimmed up his arm, a touch light enough to be playful but deliberate enough to make her intent clear. Malcolm's lips curled into a wicked smile, the kind he knew would make her blush. "Cinna," he said, letting a husky growl slip into his voice, "how could I forget you? You're the brightest star in this room. I think even the chandeliers are jealous."

Satisfaction gleamed in her eyes as she tilted her head, curls brushing against her bare shoulder. "Such a flatterer," she purred. "And I should hope you wouldn't forget me. After all, we

wouldn't want your father to think you were neglecting your future wife, would we?"

Malcolm's smile didn't falter, but it tightened slightly at the edges. He reached for her hand, lifting it to his lips with a flourish, his eyes never leaving hers. "Neglect you?" he murmured, his voice soft and intimate, the words meant for her ears alone. "Never. The very thought would keep me awake at night." He paused just long enough to let her lean in, then added, his tone deliberately suggestive, "Though I'd much prefer if you were the one keeping me awake at night."

A faint blush rose to her cheeks, high enough to be visible beneath the powdered perfection of her skin. A rush of victory surged through Malcolm—a hollow thrill, but one he leaned into all the same. This was a game he knew how to play, one he excelled at, even when his heart wasn't in it.

"You're impossible," she said with a breathy laugh, her voice warm with amusement, but she didn't pull her hand away. Instead, she tugged lightly against his grip, as though daring him to hold on tighter.

"Only because you make me that way," Malcolm said with a devilish grin, stepping a fraction closer. His voice dropped, rich with false sincerity. "What else can a man do when faced with such beauty? It's like trying to ignore the sun—you're impossible to look away from."

She laughed again, this time softer, the sound warming into something that almost felt genuine. For a fleeting moment, Malcolm wondered if there was more to her beneath the glittering façade. A secret she kept hidden behind the perfect curve of her lips and the bright sparkle in her eyes. But as quickly as the thought surfaced, he shoved it aside. He knew better.

Cinna was as much a part of this world as the chandeliers above and the champagne glasses in their hands—beautiful, soulless, and designed to dazzle. Whatever lived behind her

polished exterior had been swallowed by ambition long ago, if it had ever existed at all.

"Now you're just laying it on thick," she said, her smile playful as she reached out to toy with the lapel of his coat. Her fingers brushed the tender skin of his neck, the touch light, and she made a soft sound as if it had been a simple mistake. But they both knew the game. It was no mistake.

"And you're letting me get away with it," Malcolm countered. He caught her hand gently, his thumb brushing over her knuckles in an intimate gesture, his expression the very picture of charm. "Truly, your generosity knows no bounds. You're a marvel, Cinna. I'd be utterly lost without your benevolence."

She let out a soft, breathy laugh and leaned in just enough to close the space between them. Her perfume—a rich mix of jasmine and something faintly spicy—enveloped him as she tilted her head, giving him an unimpeded view of her cleavage.

"I suppose I should take pity on you then," she teased, her voice dropping to a conspiratorial whisper. "But you're skating on thin ice, Malcolm. Another compliment like that, and I might think you actually mean it." Her laughter rang out again, as bright as the diamonds on her ears. It was the perfect sound for this room, a sound that fit seamlessly into the glittering backdrop of shallow indulgence. It wasn't real, but it was familiar. Comfortable. Malcolm let himself fall into the rhythm of it, slipping easily into the role of the charming rake, the flirt, the man his father wanted him to be. Pretending came naturally—it always had.

And tonight, it was easier than confronting the future that loomed ahead of him.

But even as he traded quips and smiles with Cinna, his gaze strayed to Flora. The servant. She wove through the crowd with feral grace, still bearing a tray of wine glasses. Malcolm watched as she expertly dodged the questing hands of men emboldened by drink, her lips peeled back in a snarl.

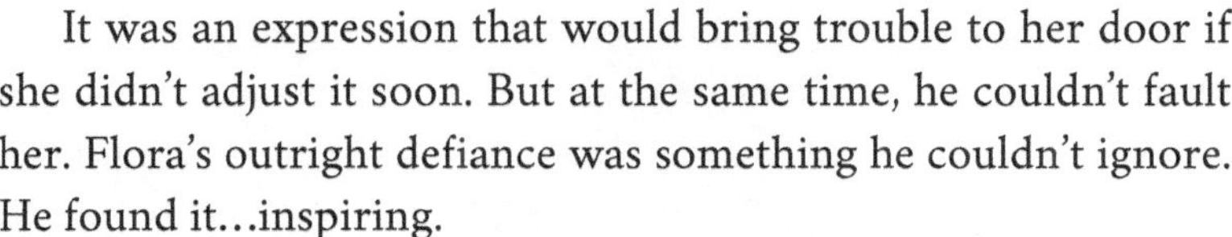

It was an expression that would bring trouble to her door if she didn't adjust it soon. But at the same time, he couldn't fault her. Flora's outright defiance was something he couldn't ignore. He found it…inspiring.

When their eyes met across the room, something passed between them that Malcolm couldn't explain. For a moment, the noise of the gala faded—the laughter, the music, the clinking of glasses all dimming to background noise, like the world itself had stepped aside to give them space.

Flora's gaze was unrelenting. So it tense it made Malcolm light-headed. It was almost as if she saw through his charade. In that moment, he felt more exposed than he ever had, as though she'd stripped away every layer of pretense with a single glance.

"Excuse me," he muttered to Cinna, distracted. He barely registered her confused response before he cut through the crowd. Flora didn't move as he approached. Her posture remained rigid, her shoulders squared as though bracing for impact. Her eyes stayed locked onto his, daring him to come closer, to meet her on her terms.

With a jerk of his head, Malcolm urged her to move away from the merrymakers. She narrowed her eyes, but followed him to the far side of a table that held the glasses of those on the dance floor.

"You shouldn't be here," he said quietly when he was close enough that no one else could hear.

"You say that like I have a choice," she replied with a snort. There was no fear in her tone, no trembling, only an edge of flippancy that caught Malcolm off guard.

His brow furrowed, and he leaned in. "You don't understand—"

But she silenced him with a look, her expression sharp enough to cut through whatever excuse he was about to offer. "Don't I?" Her words carried a quiet intensity that made

Malcolm take notice. "You think I don't see what this place is, what your family is? You think I don't know what *you* are?"

Her words stripped away another layer of the armor he didn't realize he was still wearing. Malcolm opened his mouth to respond, but no words came out. He wasn't used to anyone speaking to him like this, least of all someone of lower status.

Flora's gaze became shrewd. Her voice dropped to a whisper. "You're not like him," she said, her words thoughtful as her gaze flicked to Stafford Wells, holding court across the room. "But you could be. That's the choice you have to make."

And then she was gone. She slipped back into the crowd like a shadow, her simple gown blending into the blur of fine silks and velvet coats. Malcolm stood frozen, her words echoing in his mind.

You're not like him. But you could be.

The noise of the gala returned in full force, crashing around him like a wave. But Malcolm couldn't focus on the laughter or the music or even the warmth of the room. His mind was a storm, and he was a man seeking shelter.

Memories of his sister Alice surfaced unbidden, her laughter, her smile, the way she had so cruelly been taken away. He'd been powerless to stop it then, just as he felt powerless now.

But Flora's words remained, threading through his thoughts like a quiet refrain. A challenge. A dare.

And for the first time in a long while, Malcolm questioned who he was meant to be.

CHAPTER 2

Stafford Wells's study was a mausoleum of ambition, its walls lined with trophies of conquest: ancient artifacts, rare magical relics, and portraits of forebears whose ruthlessness had built the Wells empire.

The air was thick with the scent of leather and cigar smoke, clinging to Malcolm's skin like an accusation. He stood in the middle of the room, feeling like a small child once more. His father loomed just a few paces away, hands clasped behind his back, his silhouette framed by the flames that crackled in the hearth.

"You embarrassed me last night," Stafford said, his voice shattering the silence like the crack of a whip. He wasn't shouting—he didn't need to. "Everett Duncan asked you a simple question about the northern territories, and you answered like a schoolboy caught without his homework."

Malcolm's jaw tightened, his shoulders rigid as he stared past his father at the fire. "I told him the expansion plans were under review."

"You told him nothing," Stafford snapped, his words as hard as iron. "You stammered. You hesitated. You looked weak. Do you know what weakness invites, Malcolm? It invites doubt. And doubt, my son, is poison."

Malcolm's fists clenched at his sides, nails digging into his palms so hard they almost drew blood. He wanted to argue, to push back against his father's relentless criticism, but the words tangled in his throat. Stafford's presence had always done that—reduced him to silence, to submission, to the shadow of a man he might have been.

"I need you to understand something," Stafford continued, his voice softening just enough to make it more dangerous. "This family—this empire—was built on strength. On decisiveness. The moment you show hesitation, the moment you falter, is the moment someone sees an opportunity to take what's ours. Do you want that? Do you want to be the reason this family crumbles?"

"No," Malcolm said, the word rasping out of him like a confession.

"No," Stafford echoed, his lip curling into a sneer. "Good. Then act like it."

The heavy oak door creaked open then, sparing Malcolm from having to formulate a response. The sound drew both men's attention, and Malcolm turned to see the captain of the guard step inside, his broad shoulders filling the doorway. He shoved Flora forward, her wrists bound with iron cuffs that caught the firelight. Her pink hair tumbled in wild waves around her face, her expression carefully neutral, though her jaw tensed, the muscles tightening as though to keep her anger from spilling out.

Stafford's lip tweaked into something resembling a smile, though it was devoid of warmth. "Ah. Our troublesome new prize." His gaze swept over Flora, assessing her like a piece of merchandise at auction. "Leave her here for now, Renauld," he ordered with a dismissive wave.

The captain released Flora's arm. She tugged her arm away,

giving the man a baleful look. Renauld stepped back, pointedly ignoring her silent rage. When the heavy door closed behind him, the sound reverberated with a finality that made Malcolm's stomach tighten.

Malcolm's gaze flicked to Flora, and his heart sank. Whatever Stafford had planned, it wouldn't end well. He knew that look on his father's face—calculating, cruel, and power hungry. A part of him wished he could disappear, slip into the shadows, and avoid the coming storm entirely. But there was no escape, not for him, and certainly not for Flora.

"So, knocker," Stafford said, his voice coiling around the word like a snake around its prey. "Do you know why you were brought here?"

Flora lifted her chin, her countenance calm, but her eyes blazing with scorn. "Actually, I'm only half-knocker," she corrected, her tone light, almost conversational. "I'm as human as you are on my mom's side."

Malcolm's breath caught. Flora's words were a subtle challenge, and for a moment, the corners of her lips twitched with the satisfaction of a tiny victory.

Stafford's face darkened. For a man of his age, he moved quickly, a flash of anger given form, and then the back of his hand cracked against Flora's face. The brutal sound echoed through the room. Her head snapped to the side. Malcolm winced.

But Flora didn't stagger, didn't crumple the way so many others had under Stafford's hand. When she turned back to face him, her expression was neutral, her eyes locked on his with an unnerving steadiness. No blood marred her skin where Stafford's rings should have dug into her cheek. It was Stafford who recoiled, hissing as he cradled his hand against his chest.

Malcolm stared, struggling to mask his surprise. *Half-knocker.* Of course. The skin of full-blooded knockers was nearly impenetrable, and Flora had clearly inherited that trait.

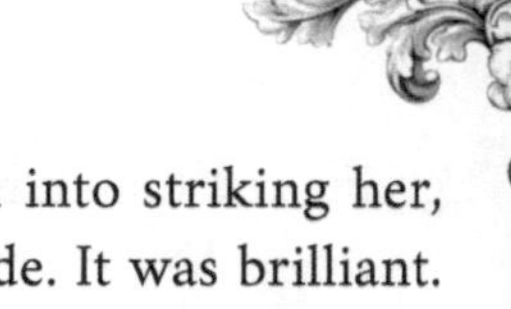

She had baited Stafford expertly, luring him into striking her, into forgetting entirely about her knocker side. It was brilliant. Malcolm bit back his reaction. If Stafford saw any hint of approval on his face…

Stafford turned away with a low growl, nursing his bruised hand as Flora stood quietly, humming a jaunty tune to herself. Malcolm shifted his weight from foot to foot, resisting the urge to intervene, though he wasn't sure what he'd even do if he could.

With a long exhale, Stafford collected himself, his shoulders squaring as if he hadn't just suffered the consequences of his own arrogance. He turned back around, his expression smooth but his eyes glinting with a dangerous edge.

"You failed to perform your duties at the Midwinter Gala," Stafford said, his tone now businesslike, detached. He paced slowly, as though regaining the upper hand with every step. "You were assigned there for a reason. To serve, to please, to enhance the atmosphere as is expected of…" He paused, his lips contorting in distaste as he searched for the word. "…a creature of your talents."

Blast. Malcolm's stomach lurched as the conversation veered back on track. He hated how Stafford reduced people to commodities, how he stripped them of their dignity with a few calculated words. He wanted to speak up, to say something, but he couldn't step out of line, not like that. Instead, he forced himself to stay still and observe.

Flora didn't cower like so many others had before her. She clearly refused to give Stafford Wells the satisfaction of fear. "I don't think anyone complained about me filling their glasses with wine," she said coolly, though Malcolm caught the faint undercurrent of venom beneath it. "Perhaps next time you should provide a script if you want your pets to recite lines."

A low, dangerous laugh rumbled from Stafford's chest, his amusement tempered by the promise of retribution. "You've got

quite the mouth on you. But make no mistake—your cleverness won't shield you from consequences." Stafford's gaze shifted, pinning Malcolm like a grasscat spotting its next target. "And perhaps my son will be the one to impress that fact upon you."

Malcolm stiffened, his breath catching. He knew immediately what was coming, and he dreaded it.

"Punish her," Stafford said, his tone casual, as though he were asking Malcolm to pass the salt at dinner. His words hung in the air, deceptively simple, but heavy with menace.

"Father…" Malcolm began, his throat dry, the word catching like sandpaper. "Surely—"

"Surely what?" Stafford interrupted, his voice rising just enough to fill the room without becoming a shout. The shift in tone was calculated, a razor's edge of warning. "You'd defy me? Over *this?*" He gestured dismissively at Flora, who stood motionless, eyes downcast. "We must keep those beneath us in line. It's critical. Not just for her, but for everyone. Strength is the only language these creatures understand."

Flora's head cocked, her gaze sliding toward Malcolm with a faint grin tugging at the corner of her mouth. Was she daring him to defy Stafford? Mocking him for his cowardice? Or was that grin her way of accepting the fate she knew was inevitable, with reckless determination? Malcolm couldn't tell, and the ambiguity of it only added to his own anxiety.

Stafford leaned closer, his voice dropping to a harsh whisper. "Do it, Malcolm. Or I'll take care of it myself. And trust me, she won't be the *only* one punished for insubordination."

The threat hit its mark. Nausea gripped Malcolm's stomach. He could argue, of course, but he knew better. His father never listened to reason, and worse, insubordination would only magnify Stafford's wrath. The consequences wouldn't stop with him. No, they would spiral outward, crushing anyone within reach, like Flora.

Malcolm swallowed hard, the memory of Flora's earlier

manipulation racing through his mind. She'd outmaneuvered Stafford once, turning his arrogance against him. If he wasn't careful, she might do the same to him. His father would see any hesitation as weakness, and weakness was a luxury Malcolm couldn't afford. Not here. Not now. No matter what he did—or didn't do—he felt trapped.

"I'll do as you ask," Malcolm said finally, his voice flat, his eyes fixed on a point just over Stafford's shoulder. He couldn't bring himself to meet his father's eyes.

Stafford smiled, his expression pure satisfaction. "Good. Captain Renauld will escort the two of you back to the dungeons. You know what to do."

The door opened immediately, as though Renauld had been waiting for his cue. He motioned for Flora to move, grabbing her arm when she didn't immediately comply. Malcolm followed in silence, his stomach knotting tighter with each step.

The walk to the garden was miserable, the crisp winter air doing little to dispel the sense of despair that had settled over him. Malcolm's gaze rested on the neatly trimmed hedges and the elegant symmetry of the topiary, a brief reminder of a world that seemed so far removed from the one he was descending into. They reached the secret entrance, a cleverly hidden passage that led to the dungeons below the estate, a place designed to contain and punish.

Renauld dragged Flora down the narrow, spiraling staircase, his grip unrelenting. She stumbled twice, her knees scraping against the rough stone, but the captain didn't pause, didn't so much as glance back to check on her. Malcolm clenched his jaw, biting back the urge to tell Renauld to stop, to give her a moment to regain her footing. Flora staggered upright with a soft curse. Malcolm's gaze dropped to her knees, noticing the absence of blood. Her skin had saved her again.

Renauld stopped at the far end of the corridor, unlocking a heavy, iron-bound door. The room beyond was simple, a

chamber designed for discipline. Malcolm fought a shiver as he stepped inside, caused as much by the below ground chill as his presence in a veritable torture chamber. Renauld shoved Flora forward, sending her stumbling into the center of the room before stepping back with a nod toward Malcolm.

"You know what to do," Renauld said. The door groaned shut behind them, leaving the two alone.

"Made your decision, huh?" Flora whispered, violet eyes narrowed.

Malcolm didn't answer. He couldn't. Any hint of hesitation, any word of kindness, and Renauld would report it to Stafford. Instead, he forced himself to move, crossing the room, though the air seemed heavy with the ghosts of past agony. The walls, streaked with stains that never quite faded, bore iron hooks from which hung an array of tools—whips, canes, and restraints —lined up like cruel decorations. Malcolm studied the instruments, gritting his teeth. His hand hovered briefly before settling on a riding crop reinforced with metal.

Behind him, Flora stood silently, her gaze burning a hole in his back. He turned, the crop heavy in his hand. That spirit still raged in her eyes, brighter than ever. It was as if she already knew what he would do—or wouldn't—and she judged him all the same. And in that moment, Malcolm felt smaller than ever, standing at the edge of something terrible, letting the world see which man he was about to become.

"Turn around." Malcolm raised his voice enough to carry beyond the thick door, ensuring Renauld would hear. His grip on the crop tightened, the leather digging into his palm.

Flora arched a brow ever so slightly, the motion almost imperceptible. She didn't say a word, but she didn't move either.

"*Turn around!*" he repeated, even louder. His voice echoed off the stone walls, his fingers gripping the crop so tightly that his knuckles ached.

Flora's gaze flicked briefly to the door before returning to

Malcolm. "So, you're *really* going to do it," she murmured, almost to herself. Her voice was knife-edged, each word cutting deeper than the last.

Finally, she turned her back to him, hands still bound in front. But there was no submission in the way she moved. Her spine was straight, her head held high. She didn't look beaten—she looked ready. Ready for what, Malcolm didn't know, but the resoluteness in her posture made him feel queasy.

"I'm doing what I have to do," Malcolm whispered. The words were meant more for himself than for her. His throat was dry, his stomach twisting into knots as he lifted the crop.

When he brought the crop down, it landed with a deafening crack—not on Flora, but against the stone floor. Dust puffed into the air as the sound reverberated through the room like a thunderclap.

Flora whirled, her eyes widening in surprise. She stared at him for a moment, her lips parted as though she couldn't believe what he'd done.

"And there's more where that came from," Malcolm announced, casting his voice toward the door.

Flora's shock melted into something sly, her lips twitching into a grin. "What are you doing?" she hissed.

"I'm doing what I must!" Malcolm bellowed, his tone theatrical as he slammed the crop against the stone again. The impact was loud enough to carry through the door. "No matter how much you protest!"

Understanding dawned in her eyes. Her grin widened for the briefest moment before she let out a piercing shriek that made Malcolm flinch. "I'll never yield to the likes of you!" she cried, her voice shaking with exaggerated fury.

Good. She understood. No prompting needed. Malcolm allowed himself a quick wink, and Flora's grin grew even broader before she schooled her expression into one of anguish. He brought the crop down again and again, the dusty floor

taking the brunt of each blow. Flora punctuated every strike with a yelp or a cry, her voice echoing as a counterpoint to the sound of the leather on stone.

Finally, Malcolm decided they had gone far enough. "Can you act like I actually hurt you?" he whispered, lowering the crop.

"Oh, can I," Flora replied, her tone laced with amusement. Then she transformed. She sagged, her shoulders drooping as though under some invisible weight. A faint sniffle escaped her as she gingerly touched her back, wincing in mock despair. She shook her head, trembling with just the right amount of misery.

Malcolm exhaled slowly, relief washing over him. He returned the crop to its proper hook, sealing the illusion they had so carefully crafted. Crossing the room, he rapped on the heavy door.

A moment later, it creaked open to reveal Renauld. The captain's eyes flicked over Malcolm before landing on Flora. "Has she been sufficiently disciplined?" Renauld asked, his tone neutral but his eyes gleaming with dark interest.

Malcolm lifted his chin, forcing his expression into one of cold indifference. "Just look at her."

Flora played her part perfectly. "He's the worst of the lot of you!" she snarled. She hissed dramatically as if in pain, clutching her side for effect.

Renauld stepped forward, gripping her arm roughly. "Let's get you into a cell to rest," he said, dragging her from the room. Flora howled, the sound so convincing that Malcolm's gut clenched. For a fleeting moment, he wondered if Renauld had hurt her, but the wink she shot him from beneath her hair as she stumbled told him otherwise.

Malcolm watched them disappear through the threshold, the heavy door groaning shut behind them. Only then did he rub his forehead, the reality of what had just happened slamming into him. He was damn lucky, and he knew it. Renauld had been

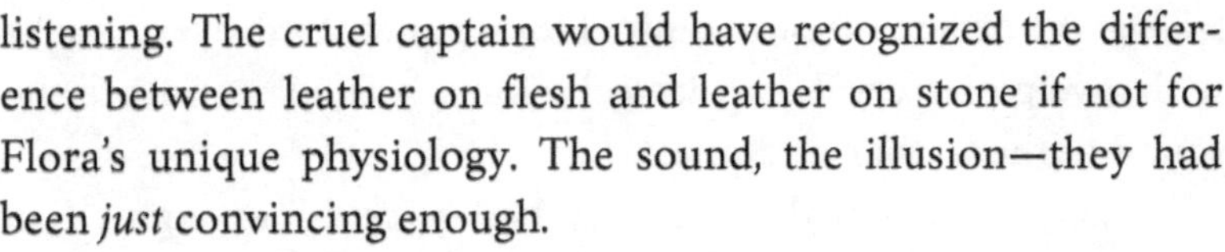

listening. The cruel captain would have recognized the difference between leather on flesh and leather on stone if not for Flora's unique physiology. The sound, the illusion—they had been *just* convincing enough.

But luck was a fragile thing, and Malcolm knew it wouldn't save him forever. If Stafford ever asked him to perform such an act in front of him…well, he wasn't sure how he'd navigate that problem.

Malcolm sincerely hoped he would never have to.

CHAPTER 3

The carriage rattled over the uneven cobblestones, jolting Malcolm with every bump and nearly jarring him from his seat when it hit a particularly deep rut. He sat stiffly on the upholstered bench, his gloved fingers tracing absent patterns along the seams of his overcoat. The chill crept in through the narrow gaps between the windowpanes and the frame, threading its way past the aging seals.

Outside, frost clung to the corners of stained-glass storefronts and the edges of wrought iron lampposts. Patches of ice glazed the street, and a damp cold settled into everything, clinging to the buildings and settling deep into Malcolm's bones. The voices of children rang out in the distance, laughter and shouts echoing faintly as they skidded on the slick pavement or tried to sculpt mounds of dirty ice into something resembling snowmen. It rarely snowed in this part of Ganland, and the stubborn frost and scattered slush were all this area had to show for the cold season.

Once, Malcolm might have smiled at the sight of children delighting in what little the winter gave them, their unbridled joy cutting through the gloom. But now, he barely registered the

scene beyond the window. His thoughts whirled endlessly, dragging him back to the memory of Flora in the dungeon and the split-second decision he had made.

When he closed his eyes, he could still feel the crop in his hand, its cold leather handle heavy with the weight of his indecision. Shame clung to him like a second skin. He had almost done it—almost struck her. And he knew he would have if the situation had demanded it, if he had no other choice. The realization turned his stomach. Each day he remained entrenched in his family's empire etched deeper scars on his soul, carving away at the man he wanted to be.

Malcolm shook his head, as if the motion could dislodge the unwelcome memory. What other choice did he have? He was a Wells. This was the life he'd been born into, the life that had been shaped for him long before he had any say in it. Malcolm adjusted his collar with agitated fingers. Today was a "training" day, Stafford had said. The condescending word floated through his mind, as though he were a dog to be schooled rather than a man struggling to hold on to some shred of humanity.

He hadn't asked what the training would entail—he knew better. Stafford's lessons weren't spoken about beforehand. They were experienced. Endured. Whatever lay ahead, Malcolm was certain it would demand another piece of his soul.

When the carriage finally ground to a halt, Malcolm briefly shut his eyes and inhaled a breath to steady himself. He quickly regretted that breath, though. The air was thick here, tainted by the smoke that billowed from the nearby factory chimneys. The processing facility loomed ahead, a nondescript monolith against the clear blue sky. To the untrained eye, it looked like little more than a collection of warehouses near the docks, but Malcolm knew better. It was a place where people disappeared.

He pulled out a handkerchief, pressing it to his nose while the stinging odor of burning coal and chemicals filtered into the

carriage. The driver opened the door, and the cold clung to Malcolm as he stepped outside.

Near the iron gate, Algernon Carroway waited with an energy that bordered on exuberant, his breath puffing visibly in the frigid air as he waved Malcolm over.

"Ah, young Master Wells!" Carroway called out, his tone cheerful. He hurried forward. "Your father said you'd be shadowing me today. An honor, truly."

Malcolm barely kept the grimace from his face as Algernon approached. The foreman's enthusiasm was infectious to some, he supposed, but Malcolm found it repellent. There was a fervor to Carroway's demeanor, an unshakable pride in his role within the Wells empire that made Malcolm's skin crawl.

"Shall we begin?" Carroway asked, gesturing toward the gate with a flourish. Malcolm nodded curtly, his gloved fingers tightening around his handkerchief as they stepped forward, the gates creaking open to admit them into the facility.

It was sensory overload. The interior was an assault on every sense, the air thick with a stench that made bile rise in his throat. Body odor, waste, and a metallic tang hung in the space, each scent vying for dominance in the balmy heat. Compared to the wintry chill outside, the place felt stifling, as hot as a forge. Malcolm stripped off his coat, folding it over his arm, though the action provided little relief.

And then there was the noise. The sound of the dungeon at the estate had been horrifying in its own right—moans, cries, and the occasional rattle of chains echoing through stone halls. But this? This was magnified a hundredfold. Chains clanged incessantly, the metallic clatter echoing off the walls. Shouts and cries overlapped into an unholy racket. The din pressed against Malcolm's skull, and he could feel the early pressure of a headache coming on.

Everywhere he looked, there were chains. They bound hands, wings, and legs, stripping the captives of not just

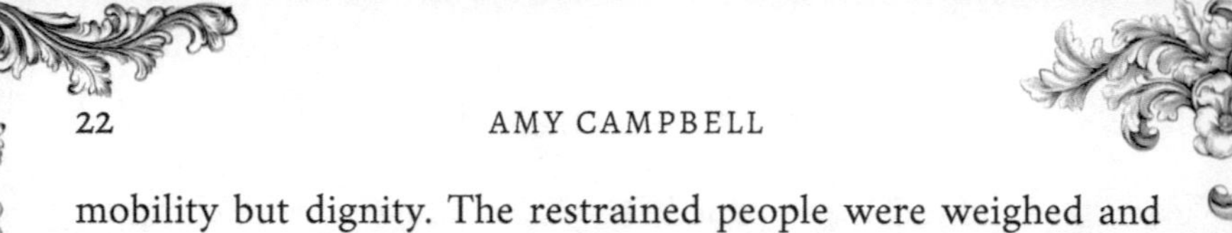

mobility but dignity. The restrained people were weighed and measured like livestock, their worth reduced to numbers scrawled in ledgers. Groups were separated and sorted with capitalist efficiency, each step stripping them further of their sense of self.

Algernon thrived in the chaos, his voice booming over the clamor as though he drew energy from it. "This is the spinal cord of the Wells operation, lad! The heartbeat of progress!" He clapped Malcolm on the shoulder with a force that made him stagger. The foreman's touch was too familiar, his enthusiasm too unbridled. Malcolm stiffened but didn't pull away. He couldn't.

"See there?" Algernon continued, gesturing to a nearby group. "Those Knossans fetch a handsome price if you can keep 'em docile during transport. Big buggers, but they're so useful for their strength. And over there—harpies!" His voice rose with almost childlike glee. "High maintenance, mind you, but their feathers are worth their weight in gold if plucked right. Now, the Theilians? Ha! Brutes, the lot of 'em. Lose half the shipment to fighting if you're not careful!"

Malcolm nodded stiffly, his gaze darting away from the foreman's eager grin. His skin crawled as Algernon rattled on.

They passed through a heavy door into an outdoor courtyard, the noise fading to a muffled roar behind them. Malcolm shrugged his coat back over his shoulders as the chill hit him again, a cold that was almost welcome after the choking stench and warmth inside. He couldn't shake the nausea rising in his gut.

Algernon prattled on, gesturing at various groups being shuffled through the yard like cogs in a machine. Malcolm forced himself to focus, but his gaze caught a scene that made his steps falter.

A scrawny knocker stumbled, the length of his iron shackles tangling his feet. His gait was uneven, his deep-set eyes

squinting painfully in the bright sunlight. Knockers were creatures of shadow and stone, their eyes ill-suited for the harsh glare of the midday sun.

"Keep moving!" barked a guard, slamming the pommel of his baton against the knocker's shoulder blade. The small man crumpled with a strangled gasp, his knees striking the dirt with a sickening crack.

Malcolm froze, his breath catching in his throat. *Do something. Say something.* But his body refused to move, his voice caught somewhere between his lungs and his tongue.

"Ahem, Mr. Wells?" Algernon's voice cut through his spiraling thoughts. "Is there…a problem?"

Malcolm's hesitation stretched for a beat too long. He swallowed hard, his mind racing. If he faltered now, it would raise suspicion. But to say nothing, to let this pass unremarked…

He cleared his throat, forcing his voice to steady. "The guards," he said, the words cold and clipped. "Tell them to fetch a shade cloth."

Algernon raised a bushy brow, his expression a mix of confusion and intrigue. Malcolm didn't falter, channeling his father's commanding tone. "The knocker. That one will be useless if it goes blind from overexposure to the sun. Protecting valuable assets should always be a priority, shouldn't it?"

A tense silence followed. Then Algernon erupted into laughter, clapping his hands together. "Ah, perceptive, just like your father! I'll see to it." He turned, giving orders to a nearby guard.

The guard sneered but obeyed, dragging the knocker out of the sun and muttering curses under his breath as he adjusted the creature's restraints. The knocker sagged into the shade, his small form slumping into the dirt with a soft, rattling exhale.

For now, at least, someone had stopped hurting him. It wasn't much. But it was all Malcolm could offer without drawing attention.

As they moved on, Algernon still prattling about profit

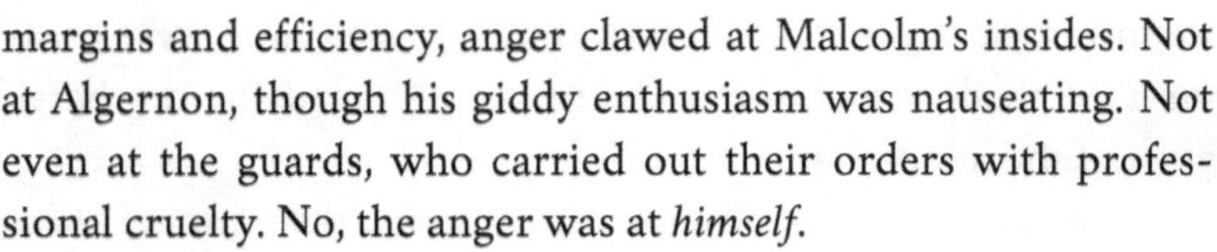

margins and efficiency, anger clawed at Malcolm's insides. Not at Algernon, though his giddy enthusiasm was nauseating. Not even at the guards, who carried out their orders with professional cruelty. No, the anger was at *himself*.

Was this really the life he was meant for? That question echoed through Malcolm's mind with every step he took behind Algernon. His thoughts churned, drowning out the foreman's voice. He was so lost in the endless loop of questions and doubts that he didn't notice the passage of time until Algernon clapped him on the shoulder and declared, with almost manic cheer, that the day was done.

The carriage ride back to the estate began its monotonous rhythm, the steady jolt of the wheels over the cobblestones doing nothing to settle Malcolm's nerves. He replayed the events of the day in his mind, each memory more horrifying than the last. His shoulders felt impossibly heavy, as though every fact Algernon had shared—every cold observation about profit margins, "asset durability," and shipment efficiency—had taken physical form and hung around his neck like iron chains.

He closed his eyes, trying to let the rumbling of the carriage wheels soothe him, but the sound only amplified his thoughts. Flora's voice drifted back to him, as though she were in the carriage beside him: "You're not like him."

And then there was Alice. Always Alice. Her memory crept in uninvited, her laughter and bright eyes cutting through the haze of guilt. What would she think of him now? The brother who had promised to protect her but now stood complicit in a system that had crushed countless others? A coward clinging to the edges of his family's evil, performing acts of mercy so small they bordered on meaningless.

The carriage jolted, its wheels catching on uneven cobblestones, and Malcolm's eyes snapped open. The manor house loomed outside, its silhouette framed against the twilight sky. Light spilled from its grand windows, creating an illusion of

warmth and invitation, but to Malcolm, they felt more like the glow of a forest fire, consuming everything in its path.

By the time the driver brought the carriage to a halt, Malcolm was rubbing his temples, trying to shake off the malaise that dogged him. He stepped down from the carriage hopeful that he could at least avoid his father for the evening.

The next morning, relief washed over him when he learned he would remain on the estate, tasked with balancing the ledgers. Numbers had always been Malcolm's refuge—orderly and consistent. Even if the ledgers chronicled the brutal efficiency of the Wells empire, they were still preferable to the horrors of the processing facility.

The ledgers waited for him in his father's office, neat stacks of leather-bound tomes arranged atop the broad desk. The room smelled of cigar smoke and old paper, the air heavy with Stafford's *presence*, even in his absence. Malcolm sighed as he sank into his father's chair, the high back and stiff leather uncomfortable. He ran his hands down his face, then flipped open the top ledger.

Stafford's impatient scrawl filled the pages, the ink heavy in places where his hand had pressed too hard. Malcolm scanned the columns, his mind slipping into the familiar rhythm of addition and subtraction, his fingers trailing the lines of figures. But today, the comfort of routine eluded him. The numbers blurred together, refusing to settle into the neat patterns he sought.

Then something caught his eye.

A discrepancy.

At first, he dismissed it as fatigue clouding his calculations. But as he traced the figures with his finger, a prickle of curiosity replaced his discontent. Food rations unaccounted for—not an insignificant amount, either. He flipped back a few pages, his brow furrowing as he noticed the same pattern. Blankets missing from the inventory. Losses tucked neatly under vague terms like *breakage* or *damage in transit*.

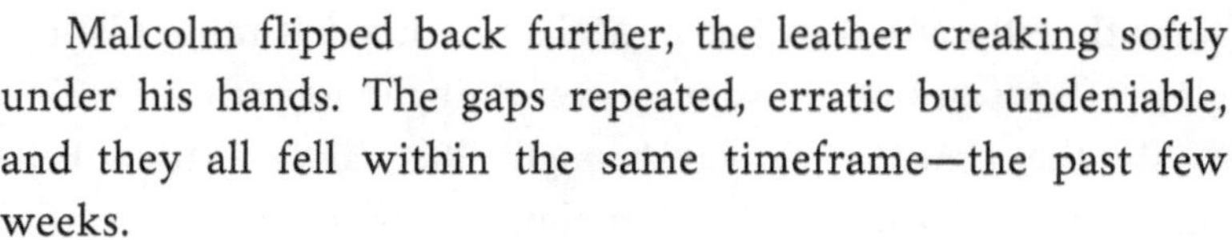

Malcolm flipped back further, the leather creaking softly under his hands. The gaps repeated, erratic but undeniable, and they all fell within the same timeframe—the past few weeks.

This wasn't carelessness. It was deliberate.

His stomach twisted as realization dawned. There was only one person who would have done this. Flora.

His mind conjured her image unbidden: the gleam of defiance in her eyes, the way she held her head high even in chains. She was weaving her rebellion into the machinery of the Wells empire, slipping through the cracks like a shadow. It was brilliant. It was reckless. And it was dangerous.

The penalties for such sabotage were severe. Malcolm knew Stafford would handle it personally if he ever caught wind of it. His father's wrath was a storm that spared no one, and Flora would be no exception. Malcolm's jaw tightened, his fingers curling into fists as he imagined the punishments Stafford would devise for her.

But then another insidious thought slithered into his mind: *What if Flora's undoing became mine?*

The evidence sat plainly in front of him, scattered across the pages of the ledgers. If Stafford discovered these discrepancies on Malcolm's watch, he wouldn't just accuse Flora. Negligence —or worse—would land squarely on *Malcolm's* shoulders. The fallout would be catastrophic for both of them.

The desk beneath his hands felt suddenly too hot, the leather-bound tomes loaded with implications. His breath quickened as the enormity of the situation settled over him.

Was she trying to get herself killed?

And in the process, was she going to take him down with her?

He leaned back with a soft exhale, forcing himself to think clearly. His father could demand to see the ledgers at any moment. The wrong answer—or worse, silence—would spell

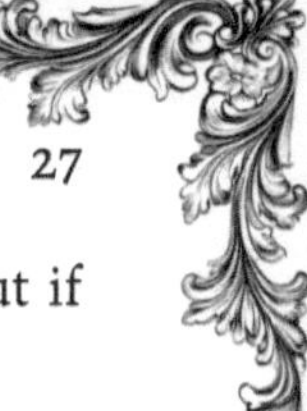

ruin. If Malcolm covered for Flora, he risked everything. But if he reported her…

Malcolm swallowed hard, his throat dry. *No.* He couldn't do it. He *wouldn't.*

For the first time, Malcolm felt the tangled vines of resistance rooting inside his chest. The sensation was foreign and terrifying, but it brought with it a hint of something unexpected. Hidden among the fear, there was…something else. A fragile hope, like the first green shoot pressing through frozen soil.

Resistance didn't have to be loud. It didn't have to be grand declarations or fiery speeches. Resistance, Malcolm realized, could be quiet. It could look like a missing blanket from a shipment. A ration hidden away. A ledger scrubbed clean of discrepancies. His lips twitched into a faint smile at that last thought.

The sound of heavy boots approaching jolted him from his thoughts. His head snapped up, heartbeat spiking as Stafford strode into the room like a storm bottled in human form. Malcolm's gut twisted as he scrambled to gather himself. He snapped the ledger shut and rose from the chair, but his father had already noticed the intensity of his focus.

"What are you doing?" Stafford demanded as he crossed the room in long, purposeful strides.

"Reviewing," Malcolm replied quickly, his training kicking in to keep his voice steady. He gestured vaguely to the stack of tomes, struggling to not tremble. "You asked me to go over the numbers."

Stafford didn't respond immediately. His dark eyes swept over Malcolm, scrutinizing him with a gaze that felt like it could pierce through flesh and bone. Then, to Malcolm's dismay, Stafford reached out and picked up the very ledger he had been poring over moments ago.

Malcolm's breath caught. He fought the instinct to reach for it, to snatch it back, knowing such a move would only invite

suspicion. Instead, he forced his hands to his sides as Stafford turned away, cracking the tome open.

The silence dragged like leaden chains. Stafford held the ledger in his hands, flipping through its pages at a maddeningly slow pace. With his back to Malcolm, he gave no indication of his thoughts, no clue to the conclusions forming in his mind. The minutes stretched on, leaving Malcolm to wish for a conclusion sooner rather than later. Best to get it done with.

"You're sloppy, Malcolm," Stafford said at last. He didn't look up, his eyes still scanning the ledger's contents. The words landed like stones. "You let mistakes linger. You allow details to slip through your fingers like sand. Sloppiness breeds weakness, and weakness is intolerable." He paused, turning the page with deliberate finality, as though proving his own point. "And now, you bury your nose in these ledgers as though cleaning up after yourself will erase the fact that you failed to notice the flaws. An heir doesn't scramble to fix mistakes. An heir ensures they *never happen.*"

Malcolm's jaw clenched. The words weren't new, but they stung all the same. He bit down on the retort bubbling in his throat, knowing better than to challenge his father now.

"You think these books will teach you how to dominate?" Stafford continued, his tone turning into a growl. With a snap, he slammed the ledger shut, the sound echoing in the room like a gunshot. "No. They *won't.* They give you numbers, yes, but numbers are meaningless without the backbone to enforce them. Without the strength to defend them."

Malcolm inhaled deeply through his nose, willing his expression to remain neutral. He had heard this speech before, but somehow, Stafford always made it feel fresh.

And then came the blow Malcolm had been expecting—but dreading—since the moment Stafford entered the room.

"Eventually, you'll need to make a choice, Malcolm," Stafford said, his voice dropping to a low growl. "Either you're the man

who ensures our legacy's survival, or you're just dead weight around my neck. There's no middle ground."

Stafford's dark eyes bored into Malcolm's, his unspoken challenge ringing louder than any shout. Then he tossed the ledger atop the desk and stepped back. Stafford moved toward the door but paused there, his hand resting on the brass knob as he glanced back over his shoulder. "Prove to me you're worthy of this family," he said, his tone colder than the frigid winds outside. "*Do better.*"

The door clicked shut behind him, the sound as final as a slammed cell door. Malcolm stood frozen for a moment, his chest rising and falling with shallow breaths. He stared at the closed door, then glanced down at the ledgers as if they were his only friend in the world.

He was alone once more.

CHAPTER 4

$\mathcal{I}$n his youth, the Wells family library had been a
sanctuary, a place where Malcolm could lose himself
in the pages of a book and live a thousand lives other than his
own. Back then, it had been an escape from his father's expectations. Now, as he stood at the threshold of the vast room, gazing
at the tall shelves stretching before him, it felt like a graveyard.
A graveyard for the man he might have become, buried beneath
the Wells name.

How could he have once read stories of heroes, those
paragons of courage and justice, while enjoying the fruits of an
empire built on cruelty? The thought made his stomach clench,
but Malcolm shook it off. He needed a distraction. And the
library, with its quiet serenity and boundless tales, would
provide it.

At least, he hoped so.

He strode into the stillness, savoring the aroma of old paper
and leather. His fingers trailed along the spines of forgotten
books, their titles faded but still legible. Here, within these
fragile pages, were echoes of lives more daring than his own:
heroes battling against impossible odds, prodigal sons seeking

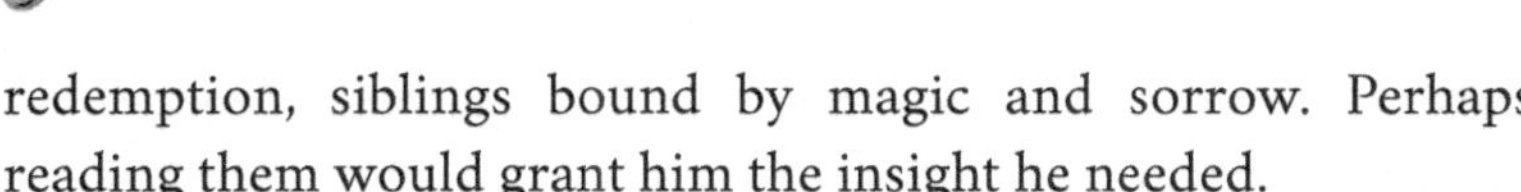

redemption, siblings bound by magic and sorrow. Perhaps reading them would grant him the insight he needed.

Malcolm paused, pulling a book at random from the shelf. He moved toward the reading area, where a cozy armchair awaited. But as he walked, a sound stopped him in his tracks.

The muffled thud of movement. The faint scrape of something heavy shifting.

A scuffle.

In the library? Everything about that was *wrong*. Frowning, Malcolm set the book down on a nearby table and followed the sounds, his pulse quickening with every step.

The noises grew louder as he approached one of the far shelves. He rounded the corner and froze, his eyes narrowing as he took in the sight before him. A section of the bookshelf had slid away from the wall, revealing a hidden passage. One of the Wells family vaults.

These rooms were off-limits, accessible only to his father. Malcolm hadn't even known there was one here. The idea of *anyone* else gaining entry was unthinkable. What was going on?

Curiosity and fear warred within him as he strode toward the threshold. The room beyond was lit by a single oil lamp. Shelves lined with stolen relics and tattered ledgers loomed inside, their contents a damning chronicle of the Wells empire's darkest dealings. His gaze swept the space.

And then he saw her.

Flora knelt on the floor at the center of the room, her vibrant pink hair a defiant splash of color in the shadows. She didn't look at Malcolm, her mouth set in a grim line as she stared at the guard towering over her.

"Caught red-handed," the guard growled. He rolled his neck before reaching for the blackjack at his hip. The weapon gleamed ominously in the lamplight, a cruel promise of pain. "Get up."

Flora didn't move. Instead, she huffed a laugh. "Or what?"

she challenged. "You'll club me back into whatever cage you've picked this time?"

The guard's fingers flexed around the handle of the blackjack. "You're too bold for your own good."

Malcolm stepped forward. "Enough." The word carried the cool authority of a man who had spent years listening to Stafford Wells, honing his tone to perfection. The sound startled the guard, who froze mid-motion and turned toward Malcolm in confusion.

"M-Master Wells?" the guard stammered, his grip on the blackjack loosening. The surge of adrenaline that had fueled him moments ago seemed to drain away in the wake of Malcolm's appearance. "This creature—she was snooping where she shouldn't be. These papers—"

"Are what I require," Malcolm interrupted smoothly, stepping inside the vault. He kept his expression cold as he stared the guard down. The man stiffened under his gaze, his posture snapping to rigid attention. "You dare to interrupt a servant I sent on family business?"

"But I—" The guard's eyes widened, his gaze darting between Malcolm and Flora as panic crept into his voice.

"Have made a dire mistake," Malcolm cut in, allowing just enough menace to creep into his tone to suggest the dire consequences of the aforementioned mistake. Then, as if catching himself, his expression eased and offered a faint smile. He took a step closer, lowering his voice as though offering a rare kindness. "But, unlike my father, I am sympathetic to your plight. You didn't know."

"I-I didn't know," the guard agreed, his lips parting nervously as he wet them.

"*Exactly*," Malcolm said, the word laced with quiet satisfaction. He had the guard where he wanted him—terrified, compliant. Somewhere in the back of his mind, he recognized that this

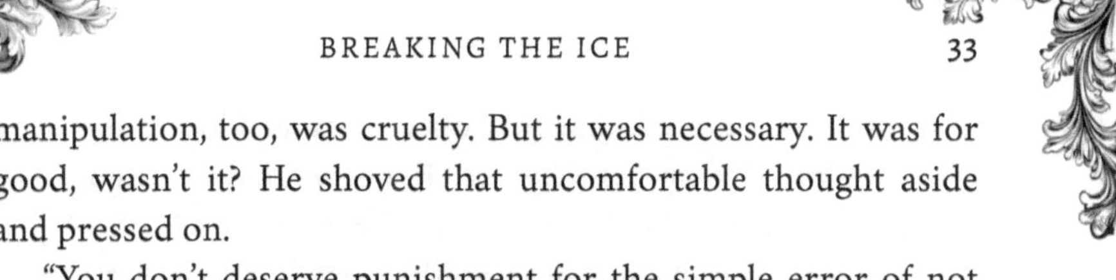

manipulation, too, was cruelty. But it was necessary. It was for good, wasn't it? He shoved that uncomfortable thought aside and pressed on.

"You don't deserve punishment for the simple error of not knowing something, do you?" Malcolm's tone turned conversational, as if inviting the guard to join him in his reasoning.

"I don't," the guard agreed, though his voice wavered. His gaze flicked briefly to Flora, who was watching him with raised brows.

The half-knocker grinned, and before either man could react, she reached out and patted the guard's arm in a mockingly reassuring gesture. "It's okay, you big lug," she said cheerfully. "We all make mistakes." Her hand landed harder than necessary, and the guard flinched as if she'd struck him. Malcolm arched a brow at the display but chose not to comment.

"I'll overlook this error in your judgment *this* time," Malcolm said, reclaiming the guard's full attention. He stepped even closer, his voice dipping lower, as though sharing a dangerous secret. "But only as long as we keep this between us."

The guard stiffened, clearly daunted by the implication. His mind was likely spinning with the horrifying possibilities— Captain Renauld's wrath or, worse, Stafford Wells himself learning of this *mistake*. When Malcolm saw the guard's shoulders relax, he knew he had won.

"Of course, Master Wells," the guard replied quickly. "That's…generous of you."

"Indeed," Malcolm said with a faint smile, wondering for a fleeting moment if loyalty could be fostered more easily through kindness than cruelty. But such an experiment was not meant for the Wells estate. He straightened, his tone turning curt. "You may return to your rounds. I won't say a word, so long as *you* don't."

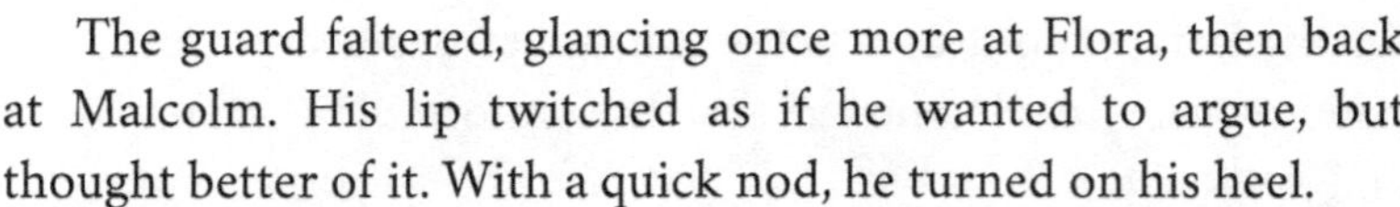

The guard faltered, glancing once more at Flora, then back at Malcolm. His lip twitched as if he wanted to argue, but thought better of it. With a quick nod, he turned on his heel.

Malcolm waited, watching as the guard retreated through the door. The vault remained open, which was fine—it couldn't be opened from the inside, only the outside. But it would provide them with a semblance of sanctuary, for the moment.

Finally, he turned to Flora. "Do you want to tell me why you're trying to get yourself killed?" Malcolm asked, his voice a strained attempt at levity. He gestured vaguely to the chaos surrounding them—piles of scattered papers, overturned ledgers, torn parchment, all lying at odd angles like the aftermath of a storm. He stepped toward her, the crunch of something broken beneath his shoes punctuating his words.

Flora's lips curved into a weary smirk, though her expression carried more resolve than humor. "Is that what you think I was doing? That I really don't have more sense than a drunk goat?"

Malcolm winced at her words, brushing a hand through his hair to feign composure. His gaze shifted to the surrounding disarray, his mind racing.

"Whatever you're doing here will only lead you to ruin," he said at last, his voice edged with frustration. "Are you hoping one of these ledgers or an artifact will be your ticket to freedom?"

Her brows furrowed, the smirk sliding away, replaced by something colder. "Don't pretend you understand what freedom is or isn't," she said, her voice low. "*You've* never had to fight for it."

The accusation hung between them, honed to a cutting edge. Malcolm clenched his jaw, the muscles tightening painfully as he absorbed the blow. Shame twisted in his chest, but it quickly shifted to irritation, a defensive heat rising to meet her challenge. "You're assuming I'm not fighting now," he said, his voice

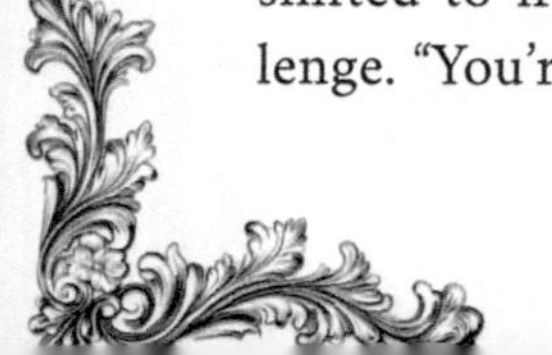

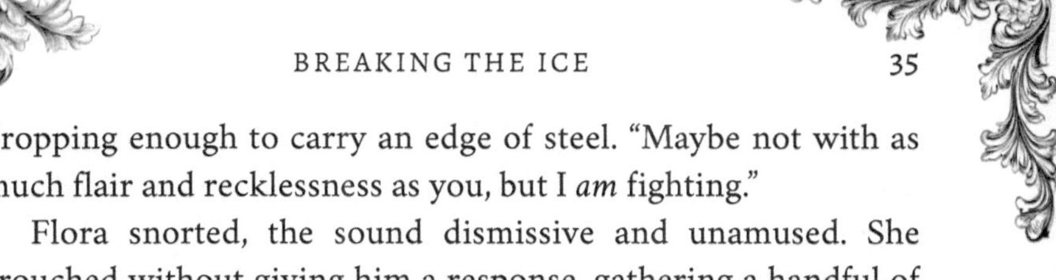

dropping enough to carry an edge of steel. "Maybe not with as much flair and recklessness as you, but I *am* fighting."

Flora snorted, the sound dismissive and unamused. She crouched without giving him a response, gathering a handful of papers from the floor, smoothing the damaged edges.

"If this is your idea of fighting, it's pathetic," she said finally, the words delivered with the casualness of someone stating an obvious fact. She didn't even bother to look up at him. "Do you enjoy playing the savior? Does it make the monster's son feel human again?"

The dismissal stung. "Do you think I do this for sport?" he demanded, crouching down to her level. Malcolm picked up a paper. "You're not the only one trapped here."

Flora rolled her eyes. "*You* could leave, couldn't you? You're not chained, not bound. So why don't *you?*"

She said it as though leaving was the simplest thing in the world. As though the empire that stretched its shadow across Ganland could simply be walked away from.

"You don't understand," he whispered, the words escaping before he could stop them.

"You're right. I don't understand a man who *chooses* to walk in chains." Flora toed at a broken shard of pottery.

The uncomfortable truth in her words made Malcolm's irritation flare. "If you hate it here so much, why don't *you* escape?" he countered, his tone harsher than he intended. "Based on the simple fact that you got into the vault, leaving the estate would be a simple matter for you." He paused, glancing at the door. "How *did* you get in here, anyway?"

"Like I'm telling *you!*" Flora huffed. "And as for why…you monsters have someone trapped here that I can't leave behind," she hissed, the bitterness in her voice raw. Then, to his surprise, Flora's armor cracked. She swallowed a lump in her throat. "My uncle."

Malcolm froze. His family had trafficked families before—it

wasn't unheard of. But this was the first time he'd faced someone directly impacted by it, someone who had looked him in the eye and named the wound.

His throat tightened, and he shifted uncomfortably, searching for something to say. He swallowed hard, choosing to change the subject rather than confront her accusation. "So what exactly are you doing here?" he asked, gesturing to the papers. "What is this? Some doomed attempt to uncover my family's hidden sins?"

Flora glanced down at the stack of papers in her hands, her fingers tightening around the edges. "I'm trying to find something—anything—that could burn this place to the ground."

The bluntness of her words startled him. Malcolm stared at her, unblinking, his mind racing to process the sheer audacity of her goal. "Burn it down?" he echoed.

"Yes. I mean, only figuratively, though the literal option is becoming more attractive by the minute," she said, rising to her feet with the sudden force of a pink-haired tornado. She stepped closer, her glare so fierce it felt like it could melt the iron rivets on the vault door. The papers in her hands crinkled audibly, but she didn't seem to notice. "You're smart," she continued, her voice gaining momentum. "I know you've seen it. The misery. The cruelty. The blood spilled by your family's hands, by *your own* complicit silence. How can you stand there and not want to raze every stone of this wretched place?"

Malcolm nearly took a step back, her passion battering against him like a relentless storm. Her words carved through the fragile defenses he'd spent years building. He opened his mouth to respond, but nothing came out. For the first time, he found himself utterly unarmed, unable to summon the justifications that had always kept him afloat in the quicksand of his father's world.

"Because I can't," he admitted finally, the words brittle as

they fell from his lips. His gaze dropped to the floor, to the fragments of torn paper scattered like fallen autumn leaves. "Because if I try, I'll drown before I can even make a difference."

Something in Flora's expression shifted. It wasn't quite pity—there was too much fire in her eyes for that—but it tempered the hard edges. She cocked her head, studying him with an intensity that made his skin prickle, as though she believed she could unravel the depths of his soul if she looked hard enough.

"You don't drown by fighting," she said at last, her voice quieter but no less resolute. "You drown by standing still, letting the tide carry you under."

Her words slid past his defenses, striking a vein he hadn't realized was exposed. He should've been angry at her audacity, at the way she spoke to him as if they were equals, as if she had any right to judge him. But there was no anger—only a simmering envy of the fire she carried, the courage to do what he could barely admit to dreaming of.

"If you keep this up," he said after a pause, "you'll get yourself killed."

Flora shrugged, and the nonchalance in her movement was almost more alarming than her audacity. "Maybe," she said simply. "But at least I'll die trying."

The silence that followed was heavy, stretching between them like a chasm. Malcolm stared at her. Questions swirled in his mind, unspoken fears pounding against the walls he'd spent years building. Could he join her in this madness? Could he defy his father in more than thought, more than these small, hesitant acts of rebellion? Or was he destined to remain a cog in the monstrous machine, spinning endlessly in the shadow of Stafford Wells?

Finally, he sighed, glancing down at the pile of papers still scattered across the floor. "What's in these?" he asked, nodding toward them.

Flora hesitated, her fingers twitching against the edge of one of the torn pages. "Evidence," she said after a moment. "Of your family's dealings with the Ganland elite. The trafficking, the bribes, the blackmail. If I can get it into the right hands…"

"Then what?" Malcolm interrupted, shaking his head, doubt bleeding through his words. "You think the Ganland elite will turn on themselves because of some papers? They'd burn you along with the documents and call it justice."

"Maybe," Flora replied. She stepped away from him, still clutching the papers, before setting them gently on the nearest table. "Maybe I'll fail. But isn't that better than doing nothing?"

"Is it?" Malcolm didn't mean for the question to escape, but it did, his voice tinged with something close to desperation.

"Yes." Flora didn't hesitate.

Malcolm didn't have a reply. The fire in her words left no room for argument, and he knew she wouldn't accept one even if he tried. Instead, he sighed heavily, his heart pulling him in half a dozen directions. "Get out of here," he said after a long pause, his voice rough. "I'll…clean up this mess. Make sure my father doesn't hear about it."

Flora didn't move immediately. She fidgeted, the slight twitch of her hands betraying the war raging inside her. "What's your game? Why are you helping me?"

Malcolm glanced at the documents on the table. "I don't know," he admitted, the honesty uncomfortable. "Maybe I just want to believe that someone can win against him."

Flora laughed—a cackle that wasn't entirely humorless. "You already said I don't stand a chance, so I find *that* hilarious." She rolled her shoulders, easing toward the door. "I better get back to my quarters and play the role of the good little servant. Let me know if your bed needs turndown service or whatever, *Master Wells*."

She paused at the threshold, turning back to face him. "I know you think you're stuck here," she said, her voice quieter

now. "Maybe it's not the chains around your neck that imprison you. Maybe it's the fear of not knowing who you are without them."

And with that, she was gone. Malcolm stood there in the silence she left behind, her words replaying in his mind long after the sound of her footsteps faded away.

CHAPTER 5

Malcolm sat on the edge of the bed, shoulders hunched, his hands clasped tightly between his knees. Sleep had eluded him for hours. Every time he closed his eyes, his father's disapproving glare bore into him. The rumble of Stafford's voice echoed in his head, each word latching on to him like a leech. He would never be enough. That much had always been clear.

He tugged at his shirt collar. His mind raced, a maelstrom he couldn't quiet no matter how hard he tried. Flora's words wouldn't leave him.

You drown by standing still.

How could she sling those words so freely, so carelessly, not realizing the depths they reached? Not realizing that Malcolm had spent what felt like his entire life doing exactly that—standing still. Watching. Waiting. Each day a numbing repetition of silent complicity, every moment a carefully measured avoidance of risk. How many times had he told himself there'd be an opportunity—a better time to act, a safer moment to defy Stafford? How many times had he promised himself he would do something, only to retreat into the shadow of inaction?

The windows rattled from a brisk winter breeze. It carried a chill into the room that sent a strand of hair into his eyes. Malcolm pushed it back absently.

He rose, pacing. The movement did little to settle the storm inside him. Flora's voice echoed in his mind, drowning out his father.

Was she right?

Was all this fear—of his father, of the world they lived in— nothing more than chains of his own making?

The thought angered him. It burned, searing through the carefully constructed walls he had built around himself. But the longer he dwelled on it, the more it made sense. And that realization left him hollow.

He slipped into a pair of comfortable leather shoes, then crossed to the door. He paused, listening for any sounds in the corridor beyond, then opened it silently.

The hallway was empty, lit by the soft glow of oil lamps. Malcolm's footsteps were almost soundless against the thick carpet as he walked. He turned a corner and stopped abruptly, realizing he was near his father's study.

Malcolm hesitated, his hand hovering just above the knob. Before he could think better of it, he opened the door and stepped inside.

The study was cold; the hearth reduced to embers that glowed faintly in the darkness. Malcolm's eyes adjusted quickly, taking in the familiar arrangement of the room—the towering bookshelves, the organized desk, the chair that felt more like a throne than a simple piece of furniture.

He strode to the desk, turning on the mage-light that stood sentinel in one corner. Pulling open a drawer, he retrieved a handful of ledgers and personal notes, stacking them neatly atop the desk. He flipped through them, his fingers skimming over columns of numbers and the handwriting that was unmistakably Stafford's.

For years, his father had taught him to catalog every decision, every transaction. But tonight, Malcolm wasn't looking for patterns or inconsistencies. He was searching for…something.

He wasn't sure what.

His fingers hesitated over an empty page. He huffed out a frustrated breath, staring at the blank page as though it might reveal an answer if he persisted.

"Fortunes of Tabris, what are you doing, Malcolm?" he muttered under his breath.

For the first time in his life, Malcolm wasn't simply following orders or retreating into silence. He wanted to act. *Desperately*. He wanted to take a step forward, no matter how small.

But he didn't know who he'd become if he tried.

What would it mean to step away from the shadow of Stafford Wells? What would it mean to leave behind the chains that bound him to this monstrous machine?

Malcolm stared at the empty page for another long moment before slamming the ledger shut. The sound echoed in the quiet room, loud enough to make him wince. He shoved the ledgers and notes back into the drawer.

Then he turned on his heel and strode back into the hallway.

THE CORRIDORS WERE SILENT, SAVE FOR THE FAINT CREAK OF THE house settling and the scuff of Malcolm's soles against the wooden floorboards. The quiet should have felt peaceful, but to Malcolm, it was just another phantom of his life in the Wells family.

He made his way toward the servants' quarters, his path taking him past the scullery. It was a space he rarely thought about, its bustling activity a mere backdrop to the estate's operations. Servants scrubbed pots, chopped vegetables, and

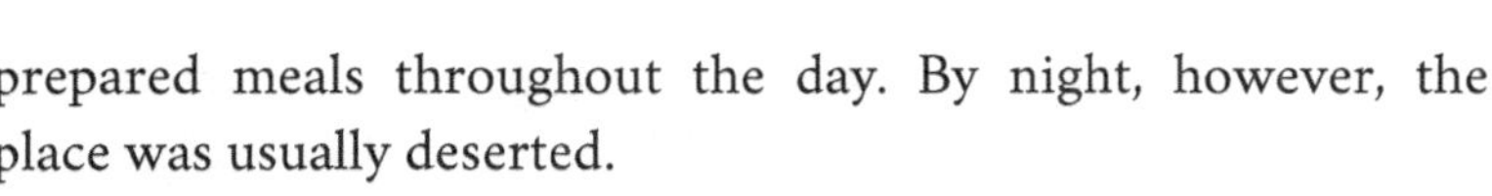

prepared meals throughout the day. By night, however, the place was usually deserted.

But as he passed, a faint sliver of light spilled into the hallway from the partially open door. He slowed, brow furrowing. The scullery wasn't supposed to be in use at this hour.

Curiosity prickled at him. It wasn't unheard of for unused spaces like this to become the site of private, often forbidden, rendezvous. Malcolm hesitated, his steps slowing. Far be it from him to interrupt anyone's late-night enjoyment. But he didn't hear the telltale murmur of voices or the rustle of movement that might have suggested such an encounter.

He cocked his head, listening carefully. Nothing.

Unable to quell his curiosity, he stepped closer and pushed the door open fully.

Inside, Flora sat perched on the edge of a lopsided chair, her boots propped on the wooden table in front of her. A wooden cup rested in her hands, her finger lazily tracing its rim as though deep in thought. She glanced over her shoulder when he entered, but didn't immediately acknowledge him; her gaze flicking back to the cup.

"If you're here to scold me, you're late," she said dryly, her tone laced with irritation. "Turns out I get enough of those lectures during daylight hours."

"That's not why I'm here," Malcolm replied, his gaze sweeping the room. It was as ordinary as he'd expected—rows of hanging pans, stacks of plates, and the aroma of root vegetables. "What are you doing in here? Looking for damning evidence among the plates and cutlery?"

She snorted, the sound rich with amusement. "Nope," she said, kicking her feet off the table. "And I'm not about to explain my clandestine workings to the heir of the Wells estate."

Malcolm winced. He had hoped his recent efforts—saving her from punishment and covering for her in the vault—might have earned a sliver of her trust. Clearly, he had been mistaken.

Still, he stepped fully into the room, letting the door swing shut behind him with a soft clunk. His hands sank into the pockets of his coat as he considered his next words.

"If you're set on burning this place down," he said finally, "you're going to need help."

That got her attention. She tilted her face toward him, her expression shifting from disinterest to incredulity. "Help? From *you?*"

"Yes."

"Oh, that's rich." She snorted again, this time leaning forward. Her violet eyes narrowed, studying him with a scrutiny that made him uncomfortable. "And what's in it for you? Guilt money? Or are we simply indulging rich-boy fantasies because you're bored?"

He stiffened at the jab, though he couldn't deny it hit closer to home than he would have liked. "Let's call it survival," Malcolm countered, his tone clipped.

She sat back slowly, skepticism stitched into every line of her expression. "Survival, huh?" she repeated, her tone dripping with disbelief. "That sounds noble. Except, last I checked, you already survive *quite* comfortably."

Malcolm clenched his fists in his pockets. He hated this dance, the endless exchange of half-truths and veiled insults. It was a game he'd been taught to play from birth, but now it felt hollow. If he was going to do this, he couldn't afford to hide behind pretense any longer.

"I'm not like my father," he said after a moment, his voice quieter now, but no less resolute.

Flora raised an unimpressed brow, her skepticism unwavering. "*That's* your sales pitch?"

"I…" The words caught like a snagged thread before he let out a tense breath. "No. It's not."

Her expression shifted, curiosity blooming across her features. "All right, rich-boy," she said. "So what is it you're

offering? I assume you've got some brilliant plan to topple your father's monstrous empire before dawn, hmm?"

Malcolm allowed himself a soft chuckle. "Not quite that ambitious," he admitted, taking his hands out of his pockets. "But it occurred to me you want to free someone. And the captain of the guard holds the key to open the dungeon cells."

Flora tilted her head, her expression dubious but intrigued. "So, what's your brilliant idea? You hold out your hand and say, 'pretty please, give me that key because I'm the heir?'"

Malcolm allowed that absurd fantasy to play out briefly in his mind, picturing Captain Renauld's reaction. It fizzled into an image of disaster, ending with the captain's mocking laughter and father's cold wrath. "You and I both know that would be an exercise in futility."

She nodded, making a little 'go on' gesture with one hand. Malcolm rubbed his hands together for warmth. It was chilly in the scullery. "As the heir, it's part of my duty to be aware of the habits of my underlings."

"How you found me here, huh?" Flora quipped.

"I'm talking about Captain Renauld," Malcolm clarified. "I have it on good authority that for an hour most evenings, the good captain is…distracted in his quarters."

The teasing light in Flora's eyes shifted, replaced by something calculating. At last, she nodded slowly, the corners of her mouth twitching upward in a faint, approving grin. "You're not entirely hopeless after all, are you?"

"Thank you for the vote of confidence," Malcolm replied, his tone wry.

"But," she continued, pointing a finger at him with mock severity, "I'm not risking myself on some half-baked idea just because *you* suddenly found your conscience. If I'm doing this, I'm doing it my way. No screw-ups. And you're not going with me."

Malcolm spread his hands in a gesture of surrender, a

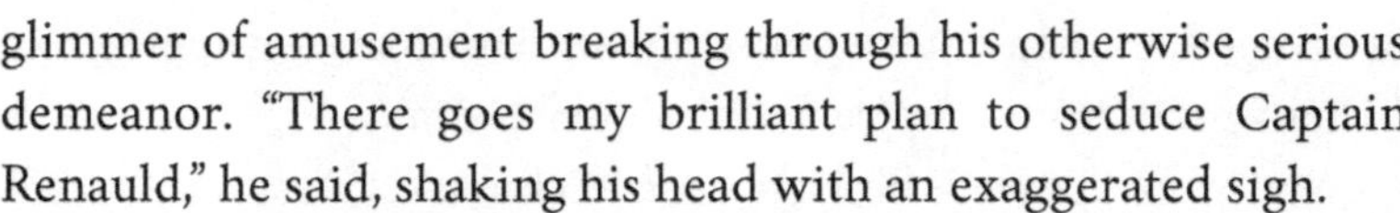

glimmer of amusement breaking through his otherwise serious demeanor. "There goes my brilliant plan to seduce Captain Renauld," he said, shaking his head with an exaggerated sigh.

She quirked a brow, her grin deepening. Then she paused, brows lifted high. "Wait, *that* was your plan?"

He grinned, his tone playful. "While the man *is* comely, he's definitely not my type." Malcolm shook his head again. "No, I was thinking more along the lines of causing a distraction. Something that would require him to leave his quarters, giving you the opportunity to retrieve the key."

"Retrieve," she repeated. "I like the sound of that. But we've gotta think this through. What are the pitfalls?"

Malcolm paused, thoughtful, his fingers brushing his chin. "There will already be guards on duty, and it would be suspect if they're not the ones to respond to the distraction."

Flora considered this, her keen mind clearly working through the logistics. Then, as if struck by inspiration, she grinned—a wicked, knowing expression that made Malcolm simultaneously admire and fear her resourcefulness. "I'll check who's on duty tomorrow night," she said, her tone light but brimming with confidence. "And then add a little something extra special to their drinks at dinner."

Malcolm gaped, his composure faltering for a moment. "*What?* You can do that?"

Flora rose from her chair and strode over to him, standing on her tiptoes to pat his cheek with exaggerated condescension. "That's a cute question." Her tone was like sugar coating a blade. "I can do *lots* of things. Don't worry your pretty head about it."

He swallowed, unsure whether to feel reassured or alarmed. Malcolm recalled how she had gained access to Stafford's vault. Yes, Flora was far more capable—and dangerous—than he or his father had expected. Gods, if Stafford Wells ever discovered what she was truly capable of… Malcolm shuddered to think of the ways his father might exploit her. Then again, Stafford's

disdain for non-humans often blinded him to their value, relegating them to servitude rather than employing them for his more insidious schemes.

Flora's gaze rested on him, her expression growing serious. "You know helping me in any way is dangerous, right?"

"I was aware of that the moment I struck the crop against the floor instead of you," Malcolm replied, squaring his shoulders. The specter of danger hanging over them didn't deter him.

Is this how you dismantle a legacy? Brick by crumbling brick?

The thought filled him with both exhilaration and dread.

CHAPTER 6

The next night arrived, its hours teetering on the edge of uncertainty. Long shadows stretched across the halls of the Wells estate. Malcolm strode through the corridors as if he were their master. And for the moment, he effectively *was*.

His father was away on a critical business trip, not to return for two days. Under normal circumstances, his mother would have assumed authority in his absence, but she had once again succumbed to her usual haze of alcohol, retreating into her chambers with a bottle of aged brandy as her only companion. That left Malcolm as the acting head of the estate. Stafford had framed it as an opportunity—no, a *command*—to prove himself.

Oh, Malcolm intended to do just that. Though not in the way his father imagined.

He sucked in a deep breath, trying to steady himself. The plan had seemed simple enough when they'd discussed it the night before. Flora had outlined her part with confidence. All Malcolm had to do was play his role convincingly, to draw Captain Renauld out of his quarters long enough for Flora to accomplish her task.

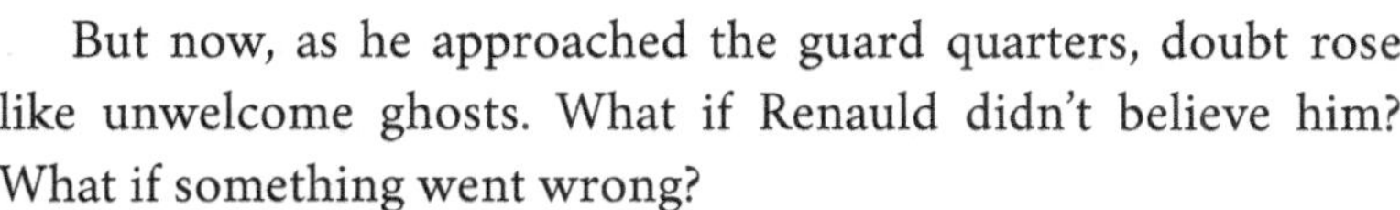

But now, as he approached the guard quarters, doubt rose like unwelcome ghosts. What if Renauld didn't believe him? What if something went wrong?

Malcolm shook the thoughts away. The plan was already in motion—Flora had assured him the guards assigned to patrol this time of night would be *thoroughly* incapacitated. Sure enough, when he'd passed them earlier, every last one had been slumped over, snoring softly with a faint sheen of drool on their lips. Whatever concoction Flora had slipped into their drinks had worked with unnerving efficiency.

Now it was his turn.

He reached the heavy oak door of the guard quarters, the building quiet save for a soft giggle and the faint rustle of straw mattresses from within. Malcolm hesitated for only a heartbeat, his hand hovering just above the door. Then, with a quick inhale, he raised his fist and pounded against the wood.

"Captain Renauld! Guards!" His voice carried an urgency that surprised even him, the tone commanding. He allowed himself a moment of satisfaction—it sounded *authentic*. "Captain, wake up! There's a disturbance in the library!"

The silence stretched for a moment, long enough for Malcolm's nerves to flare. Then came the scrape of boots against the floorboards, followed by a grumbled curse.

The door creaked open to reveal Captain Renauld, his disheveled appearance doing little to diminish the man's sheer intimidation. He was shirtless, his well-maintained physique glistening from exertion that had nothing to do with exercise. He fastened the top button of his pants, his gaze narrowing as it landed on Malcolm.

"You?" The captain's voice was gravelly with irritation. "What's this about? And what are you doing out of your chambers at this hour, Master Wells?"

Malcolm leaned into his performance, feigning frustration as he ran a hand through his hair, tousling it further. "I wouldn't

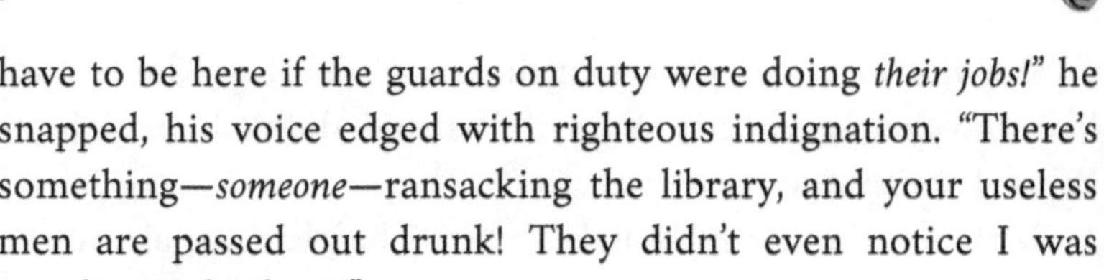

have to be here if the guards on duty were doing *their jobs!*" he snapped, his voice edged with righteous indignation. "There's something—*someone*—ransacking the library, and your useless men are passed out drunk! They didn't even notice I was standing right there!"

Renauld's expression hardened, his features contorting with fury—not at Malcolm, but at the perceived incompetence of his subordinates. "*Drunk?* On duty?" he hissed. "I'll have their hides for this."

Malcolm fought to keep the relief from showing on his face. He had him. Renauld believed every word.

"I've been hearing noises near the library for half an hour," Malcolm continued, his tone steady and authoritative. "I went to check on matters, thinking perhaps a raccoon had gotten in again. But as soon as I peeked in and saw the mess, I looked for the nearest guards. And since your men are in a drunken stupor, I had no choice but to wake you myself."

Renauld turned toward the common room next door. "You three, with me!" he commanded, pointing to a handful of off-duty guards who were already stirring from their beds. The men scrambled to their feet, clumsy as they hurriedly gathered their armor and weapons.

Malcolm watched as the guards fumbled with their equipment. Some were still rubbing sleep from their eyes.

Renauld disappeared briefly into his room, reemerging moments later with his pistol holstered at his hip and a short sword in hand. His gaze fixed on Malcolm, his expression grim. "If there's an intruder, you've no business being out here," he said gruffly. "Return to your chambers. Now. You may not be safe."

Malcolm allowed his eyes to widen, feigning surprise and fear. He clasped his hands together as though the thought had only just occurred to him. "Oh, *my!* Do you think it's assassins?"

The captain glowered at him, his patience clearly wearing

thin. "This is not the time for discussion," Renauld snapped. "With all due respect, Master Wells, you should seek the safety of your quarters. I'll post guards at your door until we know what's afoot in the library."

Malcolm forced himself not to grimace. *Babysitters. Drat.* He hadn't counted on Renauld assigning an escort. Still, he nodded dutifully, allowing a thin layer of gratitude to creep into his tone. "Of course, Captain," he said, inclining his head. "Thank you for acting so swiftly. I'll leave this matter in your capable hands."

Renauld wasted no time acknowledging the pleasantries. He was already turning on his heel. "Form up! We move now!" The guards fell into step behind him.

Malcolm turned in the opposite direction, heading toward his chambers. The soft shuffle of boots behind him confirmed the presence of two guards assigned to escort him. He bit back a sigh, maintaining the composed demeanor expected of him as the heir to the Wells estate.

As he walked, his mind raced. He was suddenly quite glad he hadn't been accompanied earlier when he'd gone to stage the library to look like an intruder had gotten inside. He'd arranged everything just so—disheveled shelves, overturned furniture, scattered books and papers—all carefully curated chaos to sell the illusion.

But this new development complicated matters. The guards following him would delay his ability to check in with Flora. He clenched his jaw, resisting the urge to glance over his shoulder at his shadows.

Patience. If there was one thing Malcolm had learned from years of living under his father's oppressive rule, it was patience. He would adapt, just as he always did.

For now, he let the door to his chambers close behind him, the faint sound of the guards shuffling into position outside a reminder of the delicate game he was playing.

Flora pressed her ear to the door outside Captain Renauld's quarters, straining to pick up any sounds from inside. The distant clamor of Malcolm's deception echoed down the corridor, but it was moving farther away. So far, everything was going exactly as planned.

The hall fell silent save for the soft hiss and occasional sputter of the nearby gas lamp. If Malcolm's ruse held long enough, she'd have time to retrieve the key and slip out unnoticed.

She wrapped her fingers around the door handle and eased it open, absolutely silent courtesy of her knocker heritage. The room was dim, shadows pooling in the corners where the light from a nearby oil lamp didn't reach. Flora wrinkled her nose at the musk of sweat, cheap whiskey, and leather polish.

Her eyes adjusted quickly to the gloom, taking in the sparse furnishings. The rumpled shirt on the floor near the bed caught her attention, though a quick check proved the key wasn't in any of its pockets. Flora's gaze flicked to the bedside table. Empty, aside from a dented mug and a deck of cards.

The key wasn't in plain sight. Either he'd tossed it somewhere in his rush, or he'd stashed it away. She'd have to search—

"Who in Tabris's name are *you?*"

The hissed words froze her mid-step. Flora spun toward the voice, her pulse spiking. In the dim light, she saw a figure sitting up in the captain's unmade bed: a young woman wrapped in a loosely draped blanket, her long brown hair mussed. The maid's dark eyes narrowed with suspicion, then widened as recognition set in.

Flora swore under her breath. She'd forgotten about Malcolm's warning regarding the nature of Renauld's nocturnal activities—had deliberately pushed it from her mind, because

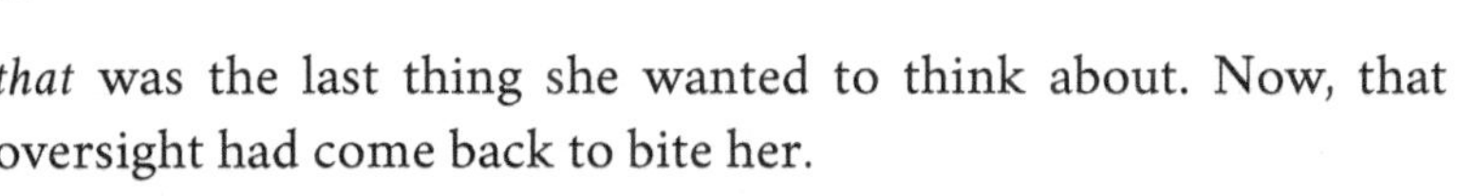

that was the last thing she wanted to think about. Now, that oversight had come back to bite her.

"What are you doing here?" the maid demanded. "This is the captain's room. Who—*wait.*" Her expression shifted as a new realization dawned. "Don't tell me. You're sleeping with him, too, aren't you?"

Flora blinked, momentarily stunned by the accusation. "What? No! That's not—I mean…" Her mind scrambled. Flora's first instinct was to deny the accusation outright, but some small, crafty part of her knew it wouldn't matter. The maid was already convinced of what she thought she'd discovered. Why not use it?

If the maid screamed now, if she called the guards and exposed Flora in the Captain's quarters, everything—*everything* —was dead in the water. She needed a way out of this, *fast.*

"Yes," she blurted out, louder than she intended. The lie tumbled from her lips before she had fully thought it through. "Yes. I'm…supposed to meet him tonight." She forced a smile that she hoped was convincing, adding with deliberate emphasis, "*Obviously.* My chunky-muscled honeybunch."

The maid's mouth fell open in shock, her face a shifting landscape of disbelief, fury, and seething jealousy. Her grip on the blanket tightened as though it were armor. "You little *harlot,*" she spat, her voice trembling.

Flora flinched at the insult but stood her ground, schooling her features into a mask of contrition mixed with indignation. "It's not what you think!" she said quickly, raising her hands in a placating gesture. But she stopped herself short. Trying to explain would only make things worse.

Instead, she shifted tactics. Her tone softened, her expression morphing into one of guilt. "I didn't know *you'd* be here." Flora injected just enough sincerity to keep the maid from escalating further.

"Oh, so now it's my fault?" The maid slid out of bed, keeping

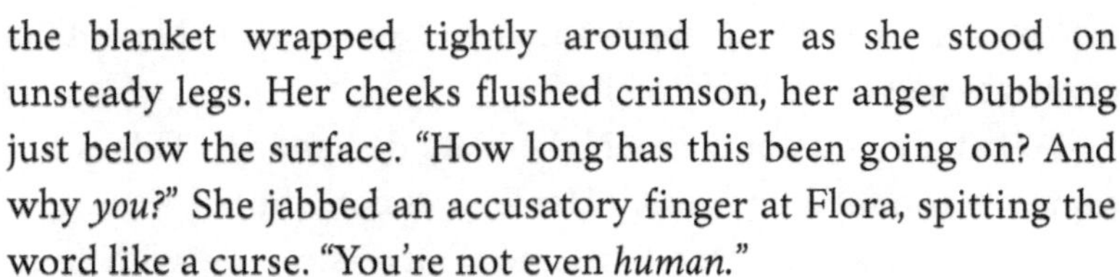

the blanket wrapped tightly around her as she stood on unsteady legs. Her cheeks flushed crimson, her anger bubbling just below the surface. "How long has this been going on? And why *you?*" She jabbed an accusatory finger at Flora, spitting the word like a curse. "You're not even *human.*"

The disdain in her voice was laughable, like being human was something to be *proud of.* Flora resisted the urge to roll her eyes so hard they might fall out of her skull. Instead, she smirked, leaning against the nearest piece of furniture with an air of complete ease. "I'm *half*-human," she corrected, her tone casual, even breezy. "And let me tell you, our captain *likes* that half." Flora waggled her eyebrows for added impact.

"Oh, I see how it is," the maid sneered. "You think being half-human gets you a free pass to hop into bed with anyone who looks your way—and with the *Captain,* no less. But you'll always be his little plaything, won't you? A dirty little secret, tucked away where no one important will see. Is that why you're skulking around here like a thief in the night? Because that's all you'll ever be?"

The words stung, sure, but Flora had heard worse—and from people with sharper tongues than this maid's. She let the insult roll off her like rain on stone, tilting her head as a slow, smug smile spread across her face. If the maid thought she could rattle her, she was in for a rude awakening.

"Oh, *sweetheart,*" Flora drawled, her voice dripping with mock pity, "is *that* what you're comforting yourself with? That the Captain keeps me a secret?" She glanced around the room, her hand flicking outward in a dismissive gesture. "Funny, because the only secret here seems to be *you.*"

Lila stiffened, her face flushing darker. "You don't know anything—"

"I know men like him," Flora cut in. "They say whatever gets them what they want. *You're different. You're special. Once I save*

enough coin." She let the words hang. "How long have you been hearing *that?*"

"You're lying," Lila whispered, but the conviction was gone.

Flora shrugged. "Maybe. But you already know I'm not." She moved toward the door, then paused. "Look, I don't care what you do with this information. Scream, tell the guards, whatever. But think about who gets in trouble if you do—and whether your captain will choose you over his position when that happens."

She slipped out before Lila could respond, closing the door quietly behind her.

Flora hurried down the corridor, retreating from the Captain's quarters like a phantom. Gods, that had been close. *Too* close.

She swallowed hard, willing herself to keep moving even as her mind replayed the confrontation. She should have accounted for this complication in Malcolm's brilliantly half-baked scheme. Renauld's nightly escapades were no secret, but the details—the *human* details—had escaped both of them. Details like an enraged maid who could have single-handedly unraveled everything with a scream.

The wall sconces cast wavering shadows across the stone as Flora rounded several corners. The faint scent of pine from the garlands strung along the corridor reached her nose, entwined with the rich bouquet of clove-studded oranges resting on a nearby table. She tried to focus on those aromas as she mulled over the cascade of events.

When Flora was certain the maid hadn't followed her, she leaned against a section of cool stone and let out a shaky exhale. For now, she'd been spared from *complete* disaster, but this wasn't over.

Her fingers flexed and uncurled at her sides like the claws of a frustrated cat. No key tonight. That much was clear. She'd have to regroup and revise her approach. Breaking in again too

soon wasn't an option—not with that maid still stewing in jealousy and suspicion.

But it wasn't just the setback itself that frustrated her. It was the maid. Her words. The sneering tone when she spat the accusation of Flora being not-quite-human.

Flora pushed off the wall and began walking again, though her pace slowed. The maid's venom echoed in her mind, burrowing deeper than she wanted to admit. No matter how much she tried to laugh it off, the insult had struck with obsessive precision, hitting a place Flora rarely let herself think about, let alone feel.

You're not even human.

Her lips twisted into a humorless smile, but it quickly faded. Was it true, then? That no one would ever look at her as someone worthy of their time, their trust, their care? That no matter how fiercely she fought or how cunningly she plotted, she would always be *other* in their eyes?

The scent of pine grew stronger as she passed a tall window decorated with a garland of dried holly berries and waxy leaves. She paused, catching her reflection in the frosted glass. The faint outline of her face stared back at her, distorted by the ice crystals forming on the surface. For a moment, she thought she saw someone else—a shadow of herself, trapped in a world where she didn't belong.

Flora blinked and turned away from the window, shaking her head as if to dislodge the thought. No. She wouldn't let the maid's petty venom burrow any deeper. She couldn't afford to. There was too much at stake, and dwelling on that bitterness would only slow her down.

MALCOLM WAITED WITH FEIGNED PATIENCE UNTIL THE GUARDS stationed outside his door finally left. The report had been

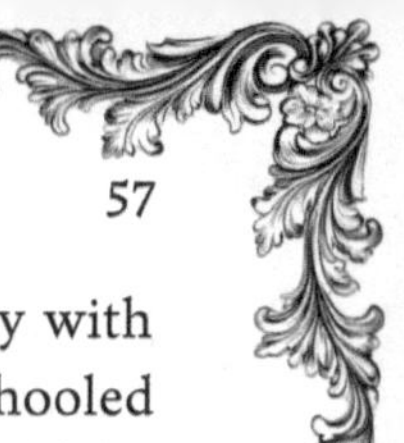

quick—no intruders, only a suspiciously disturbed library with no explanation as to how it had been accessed. He had schooled his face into a careful mask of mild concern, nodding dutifully as the guards assured him they'd increase their vigilance. Only once their footsteps had faded down the hallway did he exhale, releasing the tension that had wrapped around his chest like an iron band.

The plan had worked—or at least, his part had. But the real question remained: had she succeeded in hers?

The chill of the hallway greeted him as he slipped out of his chambers, the air brisk against his skin. He rubbed his hands together as he walked, cursing his decision to leave his gloves behind. Somewhere in the distance, the wind rattled a window-pane, the sound faint and ghostly in the otherwise still night.

The estate had fallen into its usual late-night—or perhaps early morning—hush, the echoes of footsteps and muffled voices fading into silence. Malcolm's own steps seemed unnaturally loud against the carpets.

When he entered the scullery, Flora was already there, perched on the same lopsided chair as the night before. A battered wooden cup sat beside her, its contents untouched. She stared at it like it held some profound secret she couldn't quite grasp.

The scene should have felt normal—or as normal as their situation allowed—but something was off. Flora didn't look up as he approached, though the way her shoulders stiffened told him she knew he was there. That she hadn't spun around with a smug grin, ready to gloat about her success, set his nerves on edge.

"Well?" Malcolm prompted softly, keeping his voice gentle.

Flora let out a harsh, humorless laugh, shaking her head as if she couldn't believe his audacity. "*Well?*" she mimicked, her tone derisive. When she finally looked up, her violet eyes blazed with frustration and something deeper—disappointment,

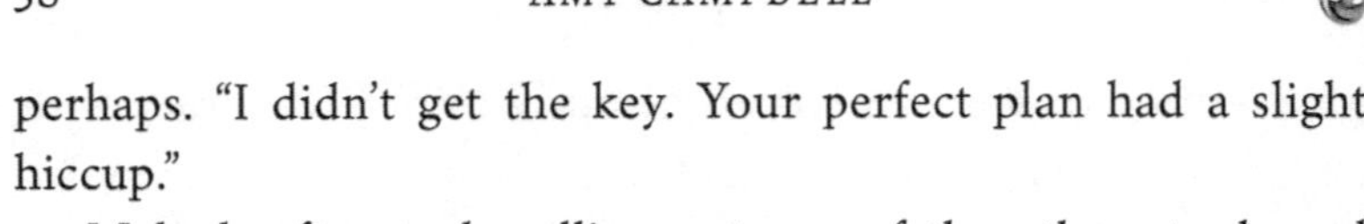

perhaps. "I didn't get the key. Your perfect plan had a slight hiccup."

Malcolm frowned, pulling out one of the other stools and sitting across from her. The wood groaned under his weight, but he didn't move. "A hiccup?" His brow furrowed.

"Yes," she said, leaning forward with a caustic grin. "Turns out there was a guest star in Renauld's little love nest tonight. A maid. She was *very* displeased to see me there."

Malcolm's stomach soured, the thrill of his earlier victory now turning into guilt. He fought the urge to bury his face in his hands. *Of course.* He'd been so focused on getting *Renauld* out of the room that he'd failed to consider the most obvious variable: who *else* might still be in the room.

"I didn't think—" he began, only for Flora to cut him off with a raised hand.

"*Obviously,*" she said flatly. Her fingers drummed a restless rhythm on the edge of the table. "We should've thought it through more. Because let's face it, if the maid had raised an alarm, I wouldn't be here right now."

A heavy exhale escaped Malcolm as he leaned forward, bracing his elbows on the table. His focus was entirely on her—on the way her jaw tightened, on the frustration radiating from her. "You're right," he whispered. "I should've accounted for that possibility. It was foolish of me to assume the room would be empty. That put you in unnecessary danger."

Her eyebrows rose at his easy admission, though the intensity in her gaze didn't diminish. If anything, Flora seemed almost disappointed by his willingness to take fault without argument, robbing her of the fight she'd been preparing for.

"I'm fine," Flora said after a beat, her tone gentler. She traced the rim of the battered cup beside her, her restless energy focused there. "She didn't raise an alarm. But…" She trailed off, her gaze sliding away, her jaw tightening as though biting back whatever she wanted to say.

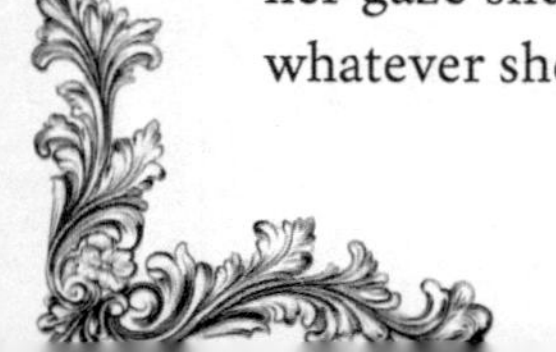

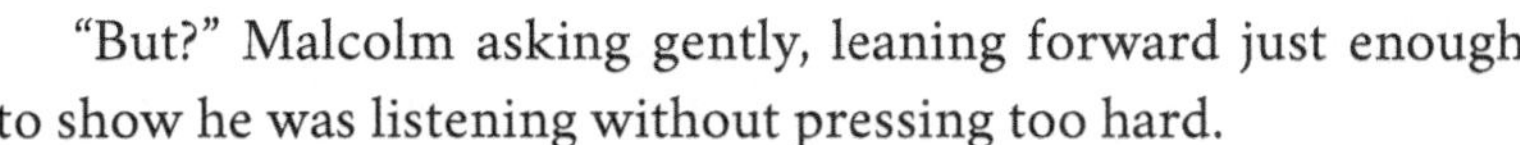

"But?" Malcolm asking gently, leaning forward just enough to show he was listening without pressing too hard.

Flora shook her head. "It doesn't matter. I just—look, it was close, alright? Too close. And that's on me as much as it's on you."

The admission caught him off guard, and he tilted his head, studying her carefully. There was something deeper lurking beneath her words. Her sharp tongue and fiery attitude were shields, but against what? He couldn't tell. Not yet.

He wanted to peel back the layers she wrapped around herself like armor, but the tension in her shoulders warned him off. Whatever haunted her, she wasn't ready to share it—not with him, anyway.

"I appreciate your honesty," he said at last.

Her eyes snapped to his, narrowing slightly as if searching for the catch. She seemed to expect him to mock her or twist her admission into some kind of leverage. But there was only sincerity in his gaze, and it caught her off guard.

She blinked, the corner of her lips twitching upward in faint surprise. "That's it?"

"That's it," Malcolm replied evenly. "You were right to call out my mistake. If we're going to keep plotting this madness together, it's important we hold each other accountable, don't you think?"

For a moment, she just stared at him, scanning his face like she was trying to decipher a puzzle. Finally, she snorted and shook her head. "You're an odd one, rich-boy. You know that?"

"So I've been told," he said with a small smile. "But I like to think it's one of my charms."

Flora rolled her eyes, though a trace of amusement crossed her features. She pushed back her chair and stretched, her joints cracking audibly. "I better get back before someone notices I'm gone. Last thing I need is Captain 'Chunky-muscled Honey-bunch' barging into my room asking where I've been."

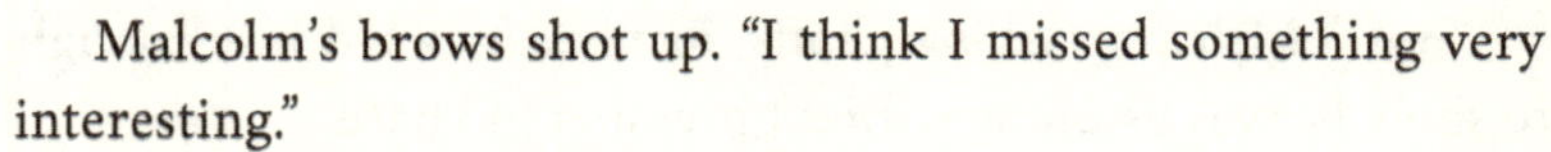

Malcolm's brows shot up. "I think I missed something very interesting."

She waved a hand dismissively, though her grin was wicked. "And maybe someday I'll even tell you about it." She started toward the door, then paused and glanced back over her shoulder. "Goodnight, rich-boy. You better get your beauty sleep, too."

For a heartbeat, her expression was unguarded—a glimpse of weariness, of something raw and unspoken. Gratitude, maybe. Then the moment passed, her expression shifting like a well-worn mask.

Malcolm understood masks all too well.

He sat in silence after she left, the scullery feeling colder without her fiery presence. Malcolm still didn't know exactly what he was fighting for—freedom, redemption, perhaps even atonement. But as long as Flora was willing to keep fighting, then so was he. Even if it meant stepping into the fire with her.

CHAPTER 7

Malcolm stood by the window of his room. His posture was rigid, as though the stillness of the frozen landscape beyond the panes had seeped into him.

The frost clung stubbornly to the trees and hedges of the estate's gardens, transforming them into glittering sculptures that sparkled in the afternoon sun. The plants wouldn't survive this. They were too accustomed to Ganland's mild winters, too fragile to endure such an unrelenting freeze. Some would wither and blacken, their delicate stems succumbing to the weight of frost. Others, the hardier ones, might emerge again from their roots come spring, tempered by the cold.

He rubbed the back of his neck, restless, as he shook his head. The rare beauty of the icy world outside felt as distant as a dream. The frost glinting on the garden paths, the shimmering lace of frozen leaves—all of it reminded him that even beauty could be cruel.

He leaned closer, his fingertips brushing the frosted glass, which stung like needles against his skin. The patterns etched by the frost seemed alive beneath his breath, shifting and disap-

pearing in ephemeral trails. His thoughts kept drifting to the chaos of the previous night, the plan that had been so neatly conceived yet so precariously executed.

The maid. He should have anticipated her presence. It was such a minor oversight, but it was enough to unravel everything. His father would have called it carelessness, further proof that Malcolm wasn't fit to bear the Wells name. The lump in his throat felt like a boulder, and he swallowed hard against it. His hand gripped the windowsill, the wood rough under his palm, as he imagined Flora caught and punished for daring to steal from the captain of the guard. And it would have been Malcolm's fault.

He sighed, leaning his forehead against the frosted pane. Why did he care so much about her fate? Flora wasn't family. She wasn't even considered a *person* in the Wells estate's ledger of profits and losses. She was an asset, a commodity. At least, that's what Stafford Wells would decree without a moment's hesitation.

But Malcolm *couldn't* think of her that way. He couldn't ignore the fire in her eyes, the way she fought against a world that sought to break her. She had courage, something Malcolm sorely lacked. She resisted with all her might, while he remained bound by privilege and duty, too afraid to risk the consequences of speaking out.

Regret and shame simmered beneath the surface, bubbling up with every memory of his father. Stafford was the embodiment of that privilege, the incarnation of all Malcolm despised about his family. His father's voice seemed to echo in his mind, dredged from a lifetime of lectures and reprimands.

"When will you finally show your worth?"

"You must not forget who you are."

"Caring for others makes you weak, boy. No one else in this world will care about you. You must look out for yourself and your legacy."

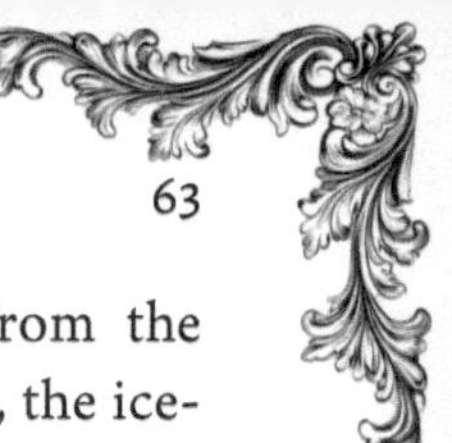

Malcolm's jaw tightened, and he pushed away from the window with a graceless, almost jerky motion. Outside, the ice-encrusted garden shimmered in the sunlight. The question weighed on him like the frost-laden branches: was he truly willing to abandon everything he knew—his wealth, his power, the comfort of his station—to stand against his father?

To stand with Flora?

He shook his head, as if to clear the thought. No. He couldn't let himself think on such notions now. There was too much to do, too many expectations to uphold. Duty called, as always.

Malcolm turned away from the window, the chill of the room clinging to his back even as he strode toward the door. He hurried down the corridor. The air smelled faintly of pine and beeswax, the aroma of seasonal decorations that should have made him feel cheerful.

Portraits of his ancestors loomed on either side of the hallway, their painted eyes following his every step. Malcolm forced himself to look straight ahead, refusing to let their imagined judgment sway him.

By the time he reached his small office in the far wing, his shoulders felt stiff and overworked, like a machine grinding to a halt. He rolled them back with a grimace. Malcolm closed the door behind him and leaned against it for a moment, letting out a gusty breath.

Ledgers, documents, and correspondence covered his desk—all neatly stacked but impossible to ignore.

He flipped through the nearest ledger absently, the worn pages as familiar as they were loathsome. Each line was a transaction, every figure a life altered or destroyed under the guise of "business." The numbers painted a grim picture of an empire that fed on misery and desperation, and Malcolm's name was etched into the foundation of it all.

How could he fight against this? He was the heir, the

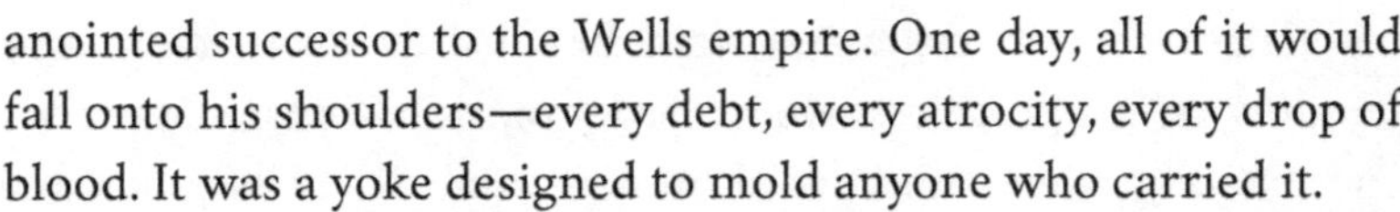

anointed successor to the Wells empire. One day, all of it would fall onto his shoulders—every debt, every atrocity, every drop of blood. It was a yoke designed to mold anyone who carried it.

Gritting his teeth, Malcolm shoved the ledger aside. The temptation to toss it into the fireplace burned at the edges of his thoughts, but he knew it wouldn't solve anything. The firelight flickered warmly against the paneled walls, offering no comfort as it danced across the leather spines of ledgers stacked high on the shelves.

A knock at the door jolted him from his thoughts. Before he could muster an invitation, the door swung open, and Stafford Wells strode in. The golden light from the hallway framed him in stark contrast, making him look like the incarnation of a god come to pass judgment.

Malcolm straightened instinctively, his shoulders squaring as if bracing against the oncoming storm. "Father," he greeted, keeping his voice neutral. "Back so early today? Your carriage must have traveled through the night. I hope your trip went well." Too soon. His father was back *too soon*.

Stafford waved a hand dismissively, his gaze keen as a hawk's. "That's a discussion for later." His tone hinted at something far more immediate. "What's this I hear about a disturbance in the library last night?"

Malcolm's stomach dropped. Of course, his father would have already heard about the incident. Nothing escaped Stafford's notice for long. Malcolm swallowed hard, keeping his face carefully composed.

"Ah, yes. That," he said, feigning casualness. "I was hoping to do some light reading, but when I entered the library, I found it in disarray. None of the guards on duty responded to my call, so I fetched Captain Renauld."

Stafford's eyes narrowed, the lines of his face deepening with suspicion. "Who found *nothing*," he growled. He stepped closer, his boots heavy against the floor like the hooves of an

angry bull. "What's going on, Malcolm? I suspect this scheme leads right back to you and your…" He let the sentence hang, his gaze dripping with contempt. "…*proclivities*."

Malcolm's jaw clenched, a spark of anger flaring in his chest at the insinuation. His father was too perceptive by half, and this was a battle Malcolm knew he couldn't win outright. He needed to disarm Stafford before the man's suspicions dug too deep.

He glanced away, allowing a hint of embarrassment to creep into his posture. "I should have known I can't hide anything from you." He forced his voice to carry a note of contrition.

Stafford's brow furrowed. "Out with it."

Malcolm's mind raced, cobbling together a story that would throw his father off the trail without raising further questions. "Well," he began, hesitating just enough to make the words seem reluctant, "at the gala a few weeks ago, I may have…accidentally arranged a romantic rendezvous between myself and a few other partners for the same evening." He cleared his throat, glancing at Stafford from beneath his lashes. "But once I helped everyone sneak in and explained the situation, they were more than happy to—"

"*Enough*." Stafford raised a hand, his expression full of disgust and irritation. "I don't need to hear any further details. I can only assume your deviance got out of hand again."

Malcolm's teeth ground together, but he forced himself to nod. "I apologize for my indiscretion."

Stafford's glare was cruel enough to pierce armor. "You need to control yourself better. Think with this," he snapped, tapping a finger against his temple, "instead of anything below the belt."

"Noted," Malcolm replied, his tone flat but deferential.

Stafford seemed ready to put the library incident behind them. He waved his hand again dismissively, as though brushing away an insignificant speck of dust. "That's not the only reason I came to speak with you. I need to discuss the

reason I hurried home." His father glanced at the chair opposite Malcolm but made no move to sit. Stafford always preferred to loom, filling the space with his commanding presence whenever the opportunity arose. "There's an upcoming meeting with a prospective buyer for some of our recent acquisitions," Stafford continued, his tone businesslike. "You're to assist in the preparations."

"A buyer?" Malcolm echoed, feigning a calm he did not feel. The words scraped against his throat, tight with unease. "Who?"

"Silas Thorncroft." Stafford's lips curled into a chilling smile, one devoid of any warmth or humor. "He was at the gala and had the chance to sample some of what we offer. He's especially interested in that pink-haired half-breed."

Flora. Malcolm's pulse spiked. Silas Thorncroft—he remembered him vividly from the gala. A man of old money, Silas had a reputation for cruelty and a volatile temperament that spared no one, least of all the "merchandise" he acquired. Anyone sent to the Thorncroft estate was essentially being handed a death sentence.

Flora might be resourceful, might be capable of turning a situation to her advantage. But Silas was no ordinary adversary. Malcolm doubted even her fire could survive being doused by the casual cruelty of a man like Thorncroft.

He forced himself to hold his father's gaze, trying to keep his emotions buried beneath a carefully constructed mask. "I see." Malcolm was relieved his voice didn't crack. "And what exactly do you expect from me?"

"I expect you to ensure that our merchandise is ready to be shown off to their best ability." Stafford's eyes blazed with impatience. "You are to oversee their presentation. Make sure everything is *flawless*. Thorncroft is not a man to disappoint."

Malcolm clenched his fists under the desk. In his mind, he allowed himself a glorious fantasy—standing up, holding his father's gaze, and refusing the task outright. He imagined the

words spilling from his mouth with confidence, imagined Stafford's shock at the rebellion.

But this wasn't a stage play. This was real life—*his* life. And in it, Stafford Wells held the reins.

Malcolm inhaled deeply, steeling himself against the merciless judgment that radiated from his father like a wildfire. "Of course, Father," he said finally, forcing the words out even as they felt like gravel scraping his throat. "I'll see that everything is ready for the meeting."

Stafford gave a curt nod, his satisfaction as bitter as the ice that had turned the estate's gardens into glassy monuments to winter's bite. "Good. I'll be expecting a report on the state of our merchandise by tomorrow evening. I trust you won't disappoint me?" His words were laden with implications, each syllable a quiet reminder of just how easily everything Malcolm cared about could be used against him.

"No, of course not," Malcolm replied, sourness threading his voice despite his best efforts to suppress it.

If Stafford noticed the edge in his tone, he made no sign. Instead, he pivoted on his heel and strode out of the room, his footsteps echoing down the hall until they faded into silence.

Malcolm remained where he was, sitting in the heavy quiet of his office as the door fell shut behind his father. His gaze fell to the ledgers on his desk, their neat rows of figures blurring together into an incomprehensible mess.

He was frozen, just like the plants encased beneath the ice in the garden—trapped by forces beyond his control, waiting for something to shift, to crack, to allow him to breathe again. But the longer he sat there, the clearer it became. He wasn't waiting for salvation. Malcolm wasn't waiting for a thaw.

He was waiting to become his father.

Fortunes of Tabris, that's the last thing I want. Malcolm closed his eyes, leaning back in his chair, as the thought settled over him like a shroud. Would the little decency that was left in his

soul wither and die beneath his father's hand? Or would it, like those plants, sprout anew in the spring—hardier for what it had endured?

For now, every breath he took made it clear he had no other choice.

But those thoughts were short-lived; the reality of preserving his situation crashing down on him. Flora would be in danger soon, at the mercy of Silas Thorncroft—all because Malcolm had agreed to stay in his father's good graces. Because he was too afraid to stand up to a tyrant.

Malcolm raked his hands through his hair in frustration. Stafford Wells was his father. And family was supposed to *mean* something.

Blood ties. Loyalty. Duty. Those things were drilled into him from the time he was old enough to understand the words. How could he dare to break away from that? To destroy that pact?

And for what?

For a half-knocker who had done little more than challenge him at every turn? For someone who had every reason to despise him and everything he stood for? Someone who would only drag him deeper into trouble with his father, deeper into ruin?

Malcolm exhaled a ragged breath, his fingers loosening in his hair as he stared blankly at the papers scattered across his desk. His mind kept circling back to Flora. For all her barbed words, she was the only person who seemed to see him—not the heir to the Wells empire, not a pawn in Stafford's grand game of power and profit, but *him*.

Or rather, who he *could* be.

That thought warmed him. Flora had glimpsed something inside him that he hardly saw in himself. Something better. Something *braver*.

His gaze drifted to the frost-covered window. Outside, the gardens lay cloaked in frost, their flowers and shrubs locked in

frozen stillness. *How like the gardens I am*, he thought bitterly. *Encased in frost, dormant, waiting for a spring that might never come.*

His lips twisted into a humorless smile. How ironic that for someone born into a life of privilege, suddenly everything felt unbearably hard. Too hard.

But maybe that was because sometimes, doing the right thing was hard.

The thought sent a ripple of something through him—determination, perhaps, or the faintest touch of courage. Malcolm rose from the desk, shoving his chair away with more force than he intended. He paced for a moment, his hands clenched at his sides, before reaching a decision.

He needed to find the schedule for the day, figure out where Flora was right now. And he *needed* to speak with her. She had to know what was coming.

At least there would be nothing suspicious about him seeking the merchandise he was tasked with preparing for Thorncroft's arrival. That would be his cover, if anyone asked.

But Malcolm wasn't thinking about Thorncroft, or Stafford, or the Wells family's damnable legacy.

He was thinking about Flora.

And what little time she might have left.

THE CHILL AIR PIERCED MALCOLM LIKE HE WORE NOTHING AT ALL as he made his way to the garden with long strides, his heavy coat pulled tightly around him. He couldn't fathom why Flora had been assigned to the garden on a day like this. What work could possibly need doing out here, with frost hardening the ground and every branch glittering under a thin sheath of ice?

He spotted her almost immediately, her vibrant pink hair almost blinding against the muted greys and browns of the wintry landscape. She was bent over a frost-coated shrub,

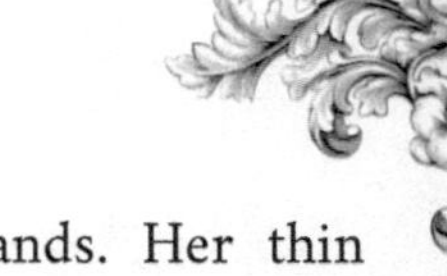

brushing ice from its branches with bare hands. Her thin servant's uniform offered no protection from the cold, and her shivering form hunched against the harsh wind.

"Flora!" Malcolm called, quickening his pace.

She straightened, turning toward him with arms crossed tightly over her chest. Her breath came in shallow puffs, and her expression was wary. "Oh, hi," she said, her tone guarded. He saw the faint trembling of her lips from the cold, but her posture still carried the temerity he'd come to expect from her.

"Why are you out here without a coat?" The outrage in his voice came unbidden.

Flora shrugged, a bitter smile tugging at her lips. "I'm just a *creature*, remember? I have stony skin, so it must mean I don't feel anything."

Her words struck him like a lash, and guilt pooled in his stomach. Without thinking, Malcolm slipped off his own coat, moving quickly to drape it over her shoulders. The garment settled over her, and she visibly stiffened in surprise.

"Here," he said, his tone brooking no argument. "Take it."

She clutched the coat around her shoulders, her body sinking into the warmth, though her skeptical expression didn't ease. "And now what? You're going to freeze so I don't? That's a real heroic look, rich-boy. I'll get blamed for that, you know."

Malcolm shook his head firmly, waving away her concern. "I'm not about to let you freeze to death out here." He hesitated, his father's voice intruding on his thoughts. If Flora got frostbite, she'd no longer be useful as "merchandise". The thought sickened him, but it gave him a justification that Stafford would accept. "Besides," he added stiffly, "Father wouldn't be pleased if the cold damaged one of his valuable assets."

Flora's lips twisted into something between a grimace and a grin. "Ah, right. The master of compassion strikes again."

"Let's go inside," Malcolm said, ignoring her jab. He gestured toward the estate, hoping she'd agree.

But Flora shook her head. "No can do. I was told to go over every single one of these shrubberies out here." She waved a hand at the frosty bushes sprawling in every direction. Her stubbornness grated on him, but he reined in his frustration. Before he could argue further, she turned to him, suspicion clouding her expression. "You never come see me during the day." Her eyes narrowed. "What's going on?"

Malcolm hesitated, her perceptiveness catching him off guard. He took a deep breath. "Flora, I need you to listen to me. I have…some news."

She turned fully toward him; the coat billowing around her like wings as she did. Her violet eyes gleamed with something between curiosity and apprehension. "What, you didn't come to read me fairy tales out in the cold?"

He shook his head, his mouth pressing into a grim line. "No," he replied. "But like some fairy tales, this one could have a horrifying ending."

Flora's pink eyebrows arched. "Oh, goody. What, am I going to turn into a glass statue like in *The Glass Garden*? Or maybe rooted in bramble like *The Thorn Bride*?" She gestured at the ice-encased bushes around them. "I should get points for making those relevant."

Malcolm rubbed both sides of his face with his gloves, hiding a strained laugh. "Yes, I'll grant you points for that." Then his expression sobered. "But this…it's serious. You caught the attention of someone at the gala."

"Oh, my *excellent* wine-pouring skills enthralled someone." Flora huffed a laugh, rolling her eyes.

"It's not funny," Malcolm said, his voice tight.

"I have to make things funny so I don't scream," Flora shot back, pulling the coat tighter around her. The fabric bunched awkwardly at her elbows, far too large for her frame. "But fine. I'll be serious. What doom awaits me, rich-boy?"

Malcolm gritted his teeth against the nickname, but let it

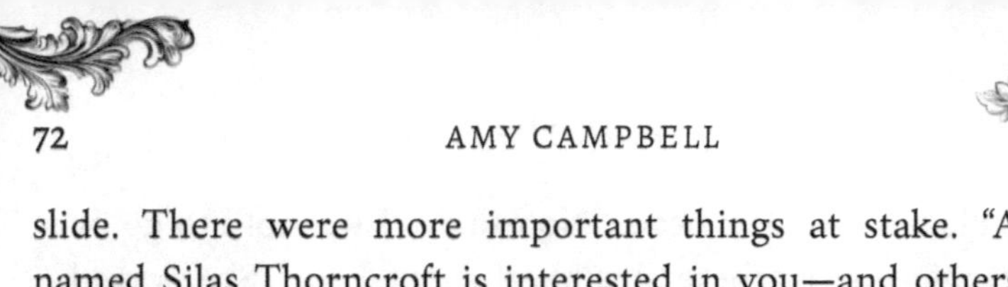

slide. There were more important things at stake. "A man named Silas Thorncroft is interested in you—and others. He's not known for his kindness."

Flora snorted, though the tension in her shoulders betrayed her unease. "Like any of you lot *are?*"

"Let me put it this way." Malcolm's throat tightened as he spoke. "Silas makes my father look like a cuddly puppy."

Her eyes widened at that, her fingers halting where they'd been brushing frost from her sleeve. "Ouch. Okay, point made." She cocked her head, studying him carefully. "So you told me. Now what?"

"I think you should escape," Malcolm whispered, glancing over his shoulder to ensure they were still alone. "That's the only way you get out of this alive."

Flora arched a brow, skeptical. "I already told you why I can't do that."

Of course, she hadn't changed her mind. Malcolm sighed heavily, his breath clouding in the cold air. A large part of him had hoped she'd agree to flee, to cut her losses and save herself, if only so his choices might feel a fraction lighter.

"What's your part in this?" Flora asked.

"I'm supposed to get you and the others prepared," he admitted reluctantly, glancing away. "To show off the merchandise to its best advantage."

"*Merchandise,*" she repeated, her tone dripping with derision. "Well, I guess that's better than being called a creature. Not by much, mind you." She shrugged off the coat and held it out to him. "Here. I think you might need this back."

Malcolm shook his head. The chill felt right somehow, as though he deserved the numbness creeping into his skin. "Keep it."

Flora sighed and draped the coat back over her shoulders. "So, what's stopping you? If you don't want to do it, don't."

Her words were infuriatingly simple, delivered with a reck-

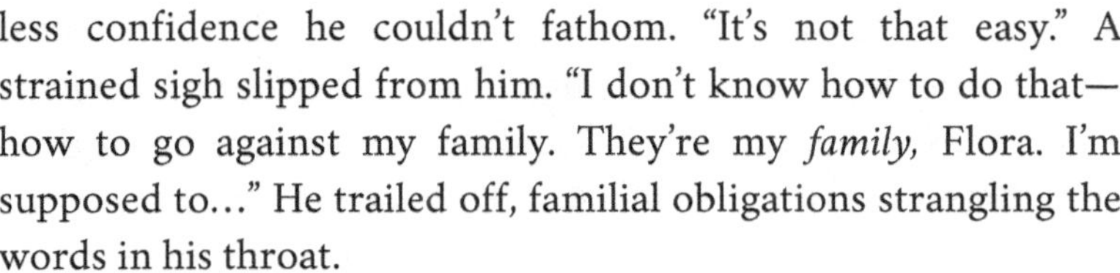

less confidence he couldn't fathom. "It's not that easy." A strained sigh slipped from him. "I don't know how to do that—how to go against my family. They're my *family,* Flora. I'm supposed to…" He trailed off, familial obligations strangling the words in his throat.

"The family that commits atrocities together stays together. I get it," Flora said dryly.

"That's not what I mean," Malcolm countered, frustration rising in his chest. He waved away the coat again when she moved to take it off, and this time she left it on. "If I don't have family, what do I have?"

Flora tilted her head, her expression becoming thoughtful. "A soul? Morals? Ethics? A spine? Take your pick." She grinned, though there was no humor in it.

Malcolm rubbed his forehead, the beginnings of a headache pulsing behind his temples. "But it's *family,*" he repeated, as if saying it again would make it mean something. "How can I plot against them when they've built this entire life for me? They—"

"Do you even consider this *life* yours?" Flora interrupted, gesturing to the frozen garden surrounding them. "Or is it just a coat handed down from one frozen heart to another?" She shook the sleeves of the coat for emphasis, her eyes boring into his. "You've been raised in a den of thieves, Malcolm—a family that trades lives like livestock. Listen to yourself. This isn't a family. Your mother's drowning in a sea of alcohol, and your father—well, he'd sell you to save face."

Her words hit too close to home. *Alice.* His father had done that to Alice. Malcolm squeezed his eyes shut, the memory of his sister—her bright laughter, the haunting music she played—piercing through his mind like a shard of glass.

"I don't have a family," Flora continued, pacing back and forth like a fierce lioness defending her territory, her words pulling him back into the moment. "Not a blood family, anyway. I lost mine when I was too young to even remember. My

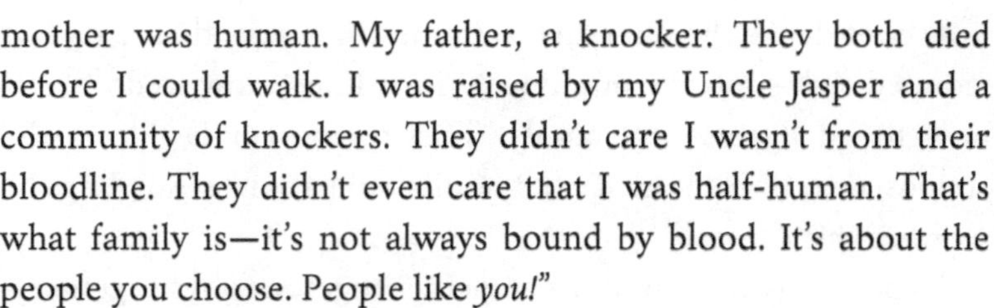

mother was human. My father, a knocker. They both died before I could walk. I was raised by my Uncle Jasper and a community of knockers. They didn't care I wasn't from their bloodline. They didn't even care that I was half-human. That's what family is—it's not always bound by blood. It's about the people you choose. People like *you!*"

Malcolm frowned. Her words were both a balm and a challenge. But there were still mountains ahead of him. "It's easier said than done, Flora. Life isn't a story, and I can't just pack my bags and leave under the moonlight. I have to consider what I'm throwing away."

"You're making excuses." Flora stopped pacing and turned to face him fully, crossing her arms tightly again. "Every day of your life has been spent tiptoeing around your father's expectations, and for what? So you can inherit a castle built of cruelty and greed? You'd rather be comfortable than have some morals?"

"*Comfortable?*" Malcolm repeated, his voice tinged with incredulity. "If you think this life of mine has been comfort—"

"Then why are you hesitating? Why are you standing here arguing with me instead of preparing to confront your father?" she cut in, her voice rising. "You're scared, aren't you?"

"*Scared?*" The word caught in his throat, bristling at the challenge. He opened his mouth, then closed it again, forcing himself to confront the truth. "Of course I'm scared! I'm standing at the precipice of my future. Every choice I make could change everything."

"Precisely!" Flora threw her hands in the air. But then her expression shifted, her eyes meeting his with an intensity that burned brighter than the wintry world around them. "And this is exactly where it begins—with you breaking free of the chains binding you." She stepped closer, the warmth of her breath ghosting from her mouth in the cold air. "You can choose what

kind of person you want to be. You can choose what you will stand for."

The words were simple, yet they hit him harder than anything his father had ever said. Malcolm could *choose*. The idea was foreign, unsettling. He'd never seen that as an option before. Had never been given it as an option. "It's terrifying," he whispered, his voice quieter now. "It's so very terrifying."

Flora let out a short laugh, breaking the tension. "Yeah, my life has been all roses so far." She hiked a thumb over her shoulder, motioning toward the bushes surrounding them. "Those roses over there, specifically. They're hardy against the frost, you see that? Kinda pretty with the ice on their petals—"

"Flora." Malcolm sighed, a faint smile tugging at his lips.

She grinned, wide and unapologetic. "You were getting too serious."

At that, he truly smiled, the heaviness in his heart lifting. "I know that you and I...we come from different worlds. But I think, if you're open to it, we could work well together."

Flora arched a brow, her grin turning quizzical. "What, are you proposing some sort of alliance?"

"Something like that," he agreed. "But different." Malcolm glanced back at the manor house, its looming silhouette a constant reminder of the chains he had yet to break. "I'll pay you a fair wage."

She laughed, the sound sudden and startling in the cold. "Did you hit your head on the way out here?"

"I'm being serious again. I know, it's no fun." Malcolm chuckled. "But Flora, I want to change things. And I think..." He hesitated, the enormity of the moment occurring to him. "I've wanted to do it for a while, but I hadn't seen a way through. Didn't have the courage to do it on my own."

At that, she nodded. "Okay, color me intrigued. How do I fit into this?"

"You seem to have a particular set of skills that make you

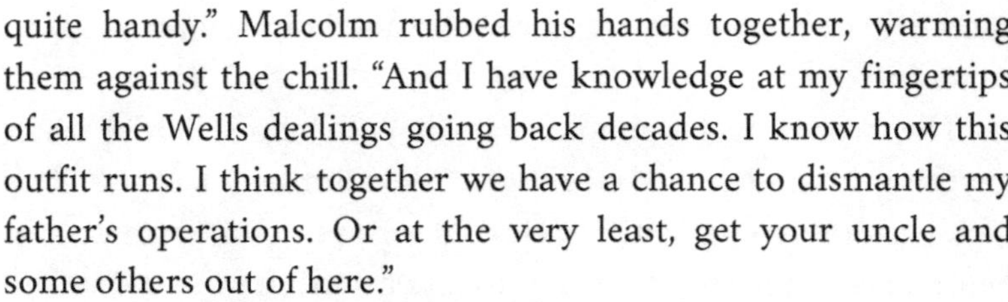

quite handy." Malcolm rubbed his hands together, warming them against the chill. "And I have knowledge at my fingertips of all the Wells dealings going back decades. I know how this outfit runs. I think together we have a chance to dismantle my father's operations. Or at the very least, get your uncle and some others out of here."

She considered this, her intense gaze never leaving his face. Then, after a long pause, she nodded. "I'm in."

CHAPTER 8

"We really have to find better places to plot overthrowing your father," Flora commented, running her index finger along the edge of a shelf at the back of the storeroom, her touch leaving a faint trail through the dust.

She wasn't wrong. The storeroom was far from ideal, the air thick with the scent of damp wood and mildew that clung stubbornly to the walls. Malcolm grimaced as he glanced around, his thoughts briefly drifting to the estate above, where the staff would soon set out the early afternoon tea service. For their purposes, this tucked-away corner would suffice.

"We could always try the parlor," Malcolm replied dryly. "Nothing like plotting treachery with a roaring fire and a decanter of brandy."

Flora snorted, spinning the knife she'd taken from the kitchen deftly between her fingers. "Sure, and we can invite Stafford for a toast while we're at it."

Malcolm couldn't help but chuckle at the unlikely mental image before returning to the task at hand. Before him, spread on an empty shelf, lay pages torn from ledgers. The Wells empire's dealings laid bare.

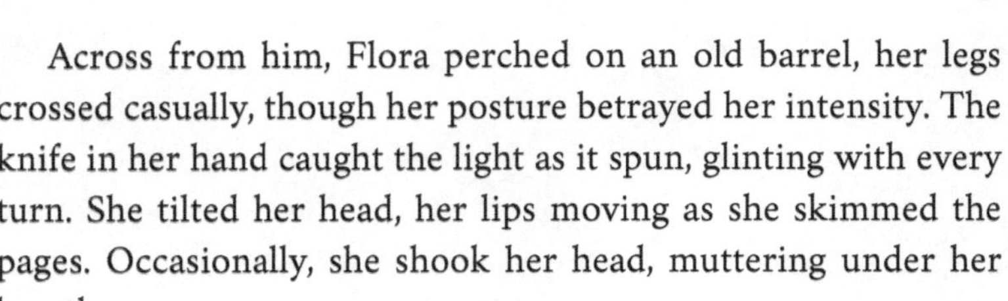

Across from him, Flora perched on an old barrel, her legs crossed casually, though her posture betrayed her intensity. The knife in her hand caught the light as it spun, glinting with every turn. She tilted her head, her lips moving as she skimmed the pages. Occasionally, she shook her head, muttering under her breath.

"So, let me get this straight," she said at last. Her voice was low, but it carried an edge. "Your father doesn't just sell people off to the likes of Silas Thorncroft. He's running half the underground network that makes sure folks like me—knockers, mages, Knossans, even humans who have the misfortune of being poor—don't get a chance to fight back."

Malcolm didn't look up. He had drawn the same conclusion as he pieced together the sordid story behind his family name. It was even worse than his father led him to believe. "That's how it appears," he said, his voice strained. "This enterprise is not just about selling. It's about *control*. Suppression. Ensuring that anyone who could upset the balance of power either works for us or…vanishes."

Flora let out a low whistle, the knife coming to a rest in her hand. "And here I thought I'd hit the jackpot when I got kidnapped by the Wells family." Her voice was laced with dark humor, but there was a hint of something else—disgust, perhaps, or resignation.

Malcolm sat back, running a hand through his hair before exhaling deeply. The ledgers felt like chains binding him to the sins of his father. "You don't need to tell me how vile it all is, Flora," he said softly, guilt threading through his words. "The more I dig, the more…monstrous it looks."

For a moment, her expression softened. Then her lips slipped into a wry smile, though it lacked its usual bite. "Yeah, well, that monstrosity's been paying for all the silk sheets and imported wine, hasn't it?"

He flinched, the truth of her words cutting deep. "I know

what I've inherited," he whispered. "And I'm trying to do something about it."

Flora studied him in silence, her gaze searching his face as though looking for cracks in his resolve. Whatever she found seemed to satisfy her. Finally, she leaned forward, setting the knife on the shelf with a soft *clink*. "All right, rich-boy," she said, her tone shifting, more serious now. "Let's focus. What's the plan for Thorncroft?"

Malcolm straightened and tapped the map spread out on the shelf. "When he arrives, my father intends to introduce him to the *merchandise*—" He winced at the word, his lips quirking as if he'd just eaten a lemon, but Flora waved a hand for him to go on. "—in the east atrium. Thorncroft will have free rein to inspect everyone, including you, before finalizing any deals."

Flora's mouth curved into a grin. "How *civilized* of him." Her voice dripped with mockery.

"Here's the thing." Malcolm tapped the map again, the sound a staccato echo in the quiet room. "The east atrium is directly connected to the servants' quarters and the wine cellars. If we can create enough chaos during Thorncroft's inspection, we might smuggle you and a handful of others out through one of the old delivery passages."

Her grin vanished like a candle snuffed out by a stiff wind. She leaned forward, glaring at him. "I told you I'm not leaving without my uncle."

Malcolm raked a hand over his face. The oil lamp flickered, casting restless shadows on the walls, and his breath hitched before he spoke. "He was added to the list." His voice dipped lower, a murmur. "Thorncroft's list."

Flora's eyes widened, the fire in them flaring to a dangerous intensity. Her mouth twisted into a snarl, though no sound escaped her lips. The knife she'd been spinning earlier now lay forgotten on the shelf. Her fingers clenched into fists so tight her grey knuckles turned pearly. "Great," she said, her voice a simmering growl. "This plan had better work, Mal. What's after the delivery passages?"

Mal. Not Malcolm. Not rich-boy. *Mal.* The name settled over him, light but strangely powerful, like an unexpected gift. It carried no weight of family or legacy, just...him. He allowed himself a fleeting smile, though it faded quickly as he refocused. "It's not foolproof," he admitted, the hesitation in his tone betraying his unease. "But it's the best chance we've got. Once you're out, you'll need to head for the forest. There's a network of paths my family's never mapped out. My sister and I used to explore them as kids."

Flora tilted her head, arms folding tighter, her brows drawing together in thought. "And who's creating this chaos?"

"I will," Malcolm said firmly, his voice steady despite the anxiety thrumming beneath his skin. He held her gaze.

Flora's brow arched. "You sure about that? Last I checked, you weren't exactly the 'distract and conquer' type." She paused. "Also, you don't exactly have a sterling record with your distractions."

There was no calculated cut to her voice as she spoke the last, but she didn't temper her words, either. Flora simply laid out the fact, a reminder of Malcolm's failure. He swallowed. "I understand your reluctance. But we're running out of options."

"Besides literally setting this place on fire." Flora rolled her eyes at Malcolm's sudden shock at the suggestion. She waved a hand. "No, no. I won't do that. Probably." She hiked a thumb over her shoulder. "The odds are too high that a bunch of innocent people would die, so I took that option off the table early on in my plans."

Malcolm nodded, relaxing a little. Flora was...unlike anyone he knew. She could speak of violence casually, as if she were discussing the weather, but she weighed every action, examining what it would cost others. As if she were performing a surgery to cut out rot.

"I've never had much practice rebelling against my father," he admitted wryly, the ghost of a self-deprecating smile flitting across his face. "But I promise I'll do my best."

Malcolm rubbed his forehead, the beginnings of a headache pulsing behind his temples. "There's another problem," he said quietly. "I need to be there when Thorncroft arrives. To ensure the distraction works, to make certain my father is truly cornered." He met Flora's eyes. "But if I show my face, if Stafford sees me interfering—"

"You'll be dragged back to the dungeons," Flora finished, her expression darkening. "Or worse."

"Exactly." Malcolm paced a few steps, his mind racing through possibilities. "What I need is a way to be there without being recognized."

Flora's brow furrowed. "You mean like a disguise? A wig and some face paint?"

Malcolm suppressed the mental image of himself in garish face paint and a wig. He shook his head. "Nothing so simple. My father knows me too well." He paused, remembering something from years ago. "There was an incident when I was younger. A rival family infiltrated one of our auctions using enchanted jewelry—glamor charms that changed their appearance entirely. My father was furious, ranted about it for weeks. He even hired a tracker and unicorn to detect such deceptions at future events."

"So get one of these charm things," Flora said, as if it were obvious. As if he could just stroll into town and pick one up at the mercantile.

Malcolm winced. "They're rare. *Expensive*. And anything like that in the estate, my father keeps under lock and key."

Flora snorted. "I think we've established that doesn't stop me."

While she was right...and it *was* tempting...it would tip their hand if she was caught, or suspected. "I don't know if

father has anything like that—and *no*, there's no need to go through secret records searching for it." Flora made a face at him. "But I know someone—a contact who specializes in...*discreet acquisitions*. They could procure one. For the right price."

"How much are we talking?"

Too much. But maybe...maybe it would be worth it. "Everything I have that's truly mine. My Fortune of Majority." All the funds he'd been gifted when he'd come of age. The Fortune was intended to start his adult life on the right foot, not...whatever this was.

Or perhaps this is exactly what it was for all along.

Flora whistled low. "That's not chump change."

"No," he agreed, tamping down the anxiety of using that much money, that quickly. "But it's the only way this works. The only way I can stand against my father without him knowing until it's too late." Malcolm shut his eyes briefly. "I'll need you to make the acquisition. I can't be seen anywhere near this type of purchase, and besides—" He offered a wry smile. "You've proven yourself far better at covert operations than I am. Could you do this for me?"

Flora stared at him. "You're trusting me with everything you own."

"I am."

She tilted her head. "I *could* take it and run. Money like that would set a girl like me up for life."

"You could," Malcolm acknowledged. "But you won't. You told me you don't leave people behind. And I think..." He paused, then continued more quietly. "I think maybe that includes me now." Gods, he hoped it did. Or he had miscalculated.

Flora snorted, but he caught the slight softening in her expression. "You're growing on me, Mal. Like a fungus." She crossed her arms. "Fine. Tell me where to go and what to ask

for. But if this contact of yours tries to cheat me, I'm stealing your fancy coat."

"Deal," Malcolm said, managing a genuine smile. "I'll get the funds tonight."

Flora rubbed her hands together in anticipation. "This contact of yours. Are they local?"

Ah, there it was. This would be where the refusal came. He swallowed. "No. She's the opposite of local." Malcolm paused, studying her. "I don't know *exactly* how you do what you do. But I *do* know that knockers can use their magic to travel certain distances."

Flora narrowed her eyes. "Right." There was a veneer of danger in his tone, like he'd just gone down a trail that led to a ravine.

"I don't need to know any of the specifics," Malcolm said, the words coming out in a rush. "But I need to know if you can get to Ravance in a timely manner."

"*Ravance,*" Flora repeated, quirking a brow. "That's an entirely different country."

"I'm aware." Malcolm's lips went taut. "I know how far it is."

The half-knocker rubbed her chin, thoughtful. Then after a moment, she nodded. "Sure. I can do that."

Malcolm blinked. "You…what? Just like that?"

She grinned. "I said what I said. It'll take a little longer than, say, running to town, but…" Flora shrugged one shoulder. "I can do it, provided no one misses me for eight or so hours."

Eight hours. Eight hours for her to span much of the conti-nent and return again. A trip that would take days even with a pegasus. As much as his curiosity plagued him, Malcolm didn't ask how she managed.

"I'll make sure of it," he agreed.

Flora studied him, growing serious again. "Fine, I'm in. But what happens if—no, when—this all goes sideways?"

Malcolm hesitated, the question sinking into him like stones in deep water. His gaze dropped to the map, then flicked back to her, his shoulders squaring as he made his choice. "If it comes to that, I'll take the fall," he said, his tone laden with finality. "I've spent my whole life hiding behind my father's shadow, Flora. If this is what it takes to finally step out of it, so be it."

Flora's expression shifted, the edges of her usual snark softening into something almost tender. For a moment, it seemed like she might say something cutting, but instead, her lips curved into a wry smile. "You're not half as spineless as I thought." Her tone was light, but carried an undertone of respect. Then, louder: "Fine. We do it your way. But if you get yourself killed, don't expect me to mourn you."

THE FIRST SIGN THAT SOMETHING WAS WRONG CAME AS MALCOLM was sliding the last ledger into his satchel. Heavy footsteps echoed down the hall. They were too forceful to belong to a servant. Malcolm's head snapped up, trading an alarmed look with Flora.

"*Schist*," the half-knocker cursed.

Malcolm swallowed, turning to Flora. "Get out of here." He *knew* she had some magic, some ability that let her move around undetected. Even if she wouldn't tell him about it.

Flora whirled, glaring up at him. "No. I'm not leaving you."

"I can handle whatever's coming," Malcolm whispered, urgent. He wasn't sure of that at all, actually. But he had been quite serious when he'd told Flora *he* would take the fall if things went wrong.

The storeroom door creaked open, the worn hinges protesting. Captain Renauld stared at them. He filled the doorway as though carved from the shadows themselves. Then Malcolm caught sight of a pretty little brunette peeking in behind him.

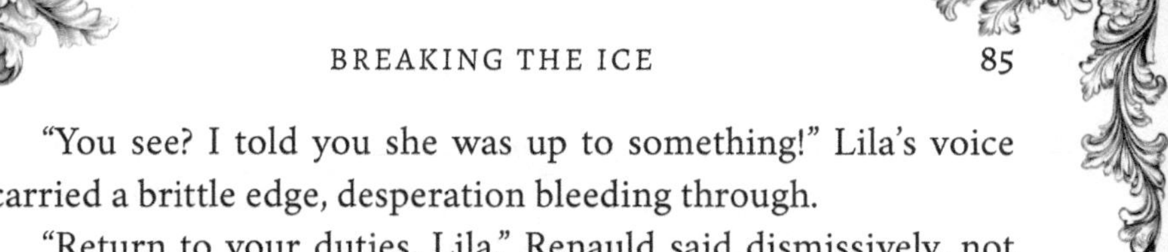

"You see? I told you she was up to something!" Lila's voice carried a brittle edge, desperation bleeding through.

"Return to your duties, Lila," Renauld said dismissively, not even looking at her. "We'll discuss this later."

"But you said—" Lila began.

"*Later*," Renauld snapped.

Lila's face fell for just a moment before she schooled it back into hopeful compliance. "Yes, Captain." She hurried away, and Flora caught the slight hitch in her step—the walk of someone who knew they were being used but couldn't afford to admit it.

The captain waited until the patter of her feet announced Lila's departure. Then he aimed a cruel smile at Malcolm and Flora. "Well, well," Renauld drawled, taking a step forward like a predator savoring the moment before a kill. "If it isn't young Master Wells and his…pet project."

Flora bristled, her hands clenching into fists at her sides. She looked as if she were one snap decision away from snatching up her knife and ripping out the captain's throat. Malcolm quickly stepped forward, positioning himself between her and Renauld.

"Captain Renauld," Malcolm said evenly, forcing his voice to remain steady even as his heart thundered in his chest. He tucked his hands into his pockets to hide their tremble. "What are you doing here?"

"I could ask you the same." Renauld stepped into the store-room, the door closing behind him with a muffled *thump*. "Though I think I already know the answer. You've been quite the busy little heir these past few days, haven't you?"

Malcolm's mind raced. How much did Renauld know? His thoughts spiraled in search of an escape, but Flora, it seemed, had no such hesitation.

"What's the matter, Captain Honeybunch?" she taunted. She leered at him, waggling her eyebrows. "Feeling left out of the big boys' games?"

Renauld's smile twisted into something darker, his gaze

snapping to Flora. He stepped closer, his boots crunching against the scattered grains of something spilled on the floor. "Careful, *half-breed*," he hissed. "Your status here is precarious enough as it is."

Flora opened her mouth to retort, her body taut like a bowstring, ready to snap. Malcolm found his voice and cut in, "What do you want, Renauld?"

Renauld's smile deepened. "Oh, nothing much," he said, dragging out each word like he was savoring them. "Just to let you know that your little escapade ends here. Your father has eyes everywhere, young master. He knows you've been... consorting with the merchandise."

"*She's not merchandise*," Malcolm snapped before he could stop himself.

Renauld's raised eyebrow spoke volumes, the glint of satisfaction in his eyes making Malcolm's blood boil. "My, my," he said, his voice mocking. "A knight in tarnished armor. How quaint." His expression hardened as he placed a hand on the pistol at his hip. He pointed to Flora. "Enough of this. You, creature, come with me. And as for you, young master, I will escort you to your father."

Malcolm's breath caught in his throat. This was it. They had been caught before they could even begin. His fists clenched at his sides, his mind scrambling for options that didn't exist. "She's not going anywhere," he said, planting his feet. His voice was firm, but his pulse thundered in his ears.

Renauld's hand tightened on his sword. "You're not a fighter, boy," he said coldly, his words like a slap. "I know the cloth you're cut from."

Not a fighter. Not a leader. A failure. The words sliced through Malcolm, his jaw tightening. His breathing grew shallow, and for a moment, he felt the room closing in around him.

Then Flora's hand brushed his arm, the light touch pulling him back from the brink. He glanced at her, and their eyes met.

Her gaze was steady, a silent communication passing between them. She knew he wouldn't stand a chance against Renauld, and more than that, she wouldn't let him try.

With a resigned sigh, Flora stepped forward, breaking the tension like the snap of a brittle branch. "I'll go," she said. "But don't think for a second this is over."

Renauld chuckled darkly. "Oh, this charade was over as soon as you conspired with the Wells heir." He stepped around Malcolm, grabbing Flora's arm. His grip was rough, his fingers digging into her skin as he pulled her toward the door. Renauld turned back to Malcolm. "Do I need to call a guard to physically escort you as well?"

The words hung in the air, dripping with condescension. Malcolm shook his head, the humiliation burning in his chest. "No," he whispered, the word barely audible.

Renauld's grin widened, a victorious gleam in his eyes. He jerked Flora toward the door. Malcolm stood frozen, his fists clenched, his mind screaming at him to do something. To step out of line for once in his life.

But he didn't.

Just like always.

CHAPTER 9

The walk through the estate's halls felt endless, Malcolm trailing in silent dread behind Renauld. Flora's smaller frame jerked against the captain's grip like a fish on a hook, but eventually, she stilled. Her chin lifted in quiet fury, jaw tight, violet eyes fixed ahead as if daring anyone to challenge her.

Malcolm's own steps faltered, his thoughts darkened with guilt and desperation. He had wanted—just this once—to do something good. Something *right*. Instead, he'd led her into this. And now, because of his failure, Flora would pay the price. He prayed Stafford's insistence on maintaining pristine "merchandise" ahead of Thorncroft's visit would shield her from the worst of his father's wrath.

As for himself? His luck had rarely extended that far.

Renauld glanced back over his shoulder. "You're quieter than I expected, young master," he taunted. "Where's all that charm and wit you wield so effortlessly at your father's side? Or has the half-breed stolen your tongue along with your common sense?"

Malcolm ignored him, his gaze fixed on the faded floral

wallpaper lining the corridor. Its pattern blurred, his thoughts fracturing as he scrambled for an angle, a way to steer this disaster into something salvageable.

Renauld took them to Stafford's study. The captain glanced at Flora as he shouldered the door open.

Inside, Stafford Wells sat at his desk, glancing up at their arrival. The room was stiflingly warm, the crackling fire more of a distraction than a comfort. Stafford was a study in control —his back rigid, hands clasped loosely before him, his face a mask of cool authority. The firelight painted harsh shadows across his angular features, an echo of the lines Malcolm now feared might one day mark his own face.

"Father," Malcolm murmured, a desperate attempt to preempt the inevitable storm.

Stafford's chilling gaze didn't shift to Malcolm, but instead settled on Flora. Renauld's rough shove sent her stumbling a step forward into the room. She recovered quickly, shrugging off his harsh shove and turning on him with a baleful glare.

"Touch me like that again," she hissed, her voice low but dripping with dark promise, "and you're gonna end up missing some key bits of yourself."

Renauld's mouth twitched, his jaw tightening as though he were swallowing a retort. For a moment, Malcolm thought the captain might retaliate, but Renauld must have known the rules. He couldn't damage what Stafford intended to sell. The thought filled Malcolm with a bittersweet sense of relief—at least Flora was safe from Renauld. For now.

"Leave us," Stafford commanded. His voice was cold and razor-edged, a tone Malcolm had learned early never to question.

Renauld hesitated for the briefest moment before stepping back with a stiff nod. "As you wish." He cast a final smug glance at Malcolm before retreating, the heavy doors drawing shut behind him with a sound that seemed to seal their fate.

The silence that followed was absolute, broken only by the occasional crack and hiss of the fire. Stafford let the quiet stretch, his steepled fingers resting beneath his chin as his gaze rested on Flora before finally sliding to Malcolm.

"You've disappointed me before," Stafford began, his tone calm in a way that sent a shiver down Malcolm's spine. That frigid calm was always worse than shouting—it was the quiet before the lash, the prelude to punishment. "But this…*this* is a new low."

"Father, I—" Malcolm tried, his voice faltering as he took a step forward.

Stafford raised a hand, cutting him off mid-sentence. "*Quiet.*" Malcolm stopped immediately, swallowing hard as the room seemed to shrink around him.

Stafford turned his attention to Flora again, his lips curling into a sneer. "And *you*," he said with disgust. "I don't know what sort of con you're running, creature, but you've made a grave mistake involving yourself in my son's idiocy. Not that I'm surprised—he's always been one to think with the organ below the belt rather than the one in his head."

Malcolm's teeth grated at the insult. But instead of responding, he bowed his head, his hands trembling at his sides. He felt helpless, reduced to nothing more than a child standing in his father's overwhelming shadow.

Flora, however, was not one to bow. She straightened, cocking her head in mock consideration. "If your son's an idiot," she said sweetly, with a saccharine tone that couldn't mask the calculated strike beneath, "what does that make you?"

Malcolm's heart dropped. His head snapped up, and he stared at her, silently begging her to stop. She was going to make herself a target, and that was the last thing he wanted. "*Flora,*" he whispered, but she didn't acknowledge him.

Stafford's eyes narrowed dangerously, the muscles in his jaw

tightening. His tone dropped, colder now. "I see the half-breed doesn't know her place."

"She has nothing to do with this!" Malcolm blurted, stepping forward. He had to protect her, had to take the focus off her bold tongue. "Father, please—"

"*Nothing to do with this?*" Stafford repeated mockingly, snapping his attention to Malcolm. His derisive laugh echoed off the wooden beams of the ceiling. "I should think she has *everything* to do with this. Or are you suggesting I'm mistaken about your little escapades with the merchandise?"

Malcolm flinched at the word but held his ground. "Father, I—"

"Do you think you *love* her, Malcolm?" The question was sudden, cutting through the room with surgical precision. Stafford's question wasn't curious; it was an accusation. A trap.

Malcolm froze, his mind racing. *Love?* The word felt foreign, too weighted for what he understood of his feelings. He didn't know what he felt—respect? Admiration? A desperate need to see her safe? It wasn't what his father was implying, but it was something.

"I…" The word faltered on his tongue. He couldn't find an answer.

"You don't even know, do you?" Stafford scoffed, rising to his full height. Behind him, the fire flared, casting him in an unearthly glow. "Do you know what I see when I look at you, Malcolm? Weakness. I've told you before what love is: a vulnerability. A leash. And here you are, letting yourself be distracted and manipulated by trash who should know their place."

Flora stiffened. Her glare burned into Stafford with the intensity of an inferno, but he didn't so much as glance at her. Malcolm glanced toward her, searching for her knife. Was it still back in the storeroom?

Stafford stepped closer to his son, looming over him. "Do you think this rebellion of yours will earn you redemption? Do

you think these…attachments make you *noble?*" He laughed. "They don't. They make you a *fool.*"

Malcolm trembled, but he forced himself to speak. "Father, I'm not trying to—"

"*Silence.*" Stafford's voice cracked like a whip, but Malcolm squared his shoulders, drawing on a surge of courage that surprised even him.

"This operation—it's *wrong,*" Malcolm said, raising his voice. "What we're doing, what you're doing, it's *monstrous.*"

Stafford stopped, his gaze narrowing dangerously. "*Monstrous?*" he repeated, incredulous. "You dare to judge me? Everything you have—your comfort, your privilege, your safety —exists because of what I've built. Because of what this *family* has built."

"I don't want it," Malcolm said fiercely, the words escaping before he could think better of them.

Stafford's eyes widened for a beat, then hardened. Before Malcolm could react, his father closed the distance between them. Stafford's hand lashed out, the back of it striking Malcolm across the face with enough force to send him staggering. Malcolm crashed into the side of the desk, catching himself on the edge. Stinging pain bloomed across his cheek and the metallic tang of blood filled his mouth.

"*Enough,*" Stafford growled, standing over him like a dark tower. "You will fall in line, Malcolm. Or you will fall."

Malcolm pressed a hand to his face, his vision blurring. He felt Flora move beside him, but before she did anything, Stafford's words rooted her in place.

"I wouldn't, if I were you," he warned, his tone deathly calm. "Your intervention isn't doing him any favors."

Flora froze, her boldness dulling into caution. Her gaze fell on him, her violet eyes wide with something unexpected: worry.

Worry for *him.*

Malcolm's breath hitched. No one had ever looked at him like that before. No one had ever cared enough to.

"Renauld! Take her to the dungeon," Stafford barked.

The doors groaned open again, and Renauld entered, his expression keen with a sickening eagerness. He grabbed Flora's arm without hesitation, hauling her toward the door. She didn't fight—not outwardly—but the tension in her frame, the way her jaw tightened, spoke volumes.

Malcolm struggled to his feet, swaying as he did so. His cheek throbbed from where Stafford had struck him, and his legs felt unsteady beneath him. But he couldn't just stand there and let this happen. He opened his mouth to protest, to shout, to do something—*anything*.

But what could he do? He could barely stand, let alone face down Renauld or his father. The truth that Renauld had spat earlier echoed in his mind: *You're not a fighter, boy.*

And he wasn't.

The door slammed shut behind Renauld and Flora. Malcolm stared at the door, anger and helplessness swirling inside him.

He was alone with his father now.

For a long moment, neither of them spoke. Stafford moved back to his desk with an air of utter indifference, sitting down as if nothing had transpired. The casual way he rested his hands on the polished surface of the desk, steepling his fingers, made Malcolm's stomach drop.

Stafford finally broke the silence. "Since you're currently compromised, I'm removing you from the Thorncroft job."

The words hit Malcolm like a punch to the gut, even though he had expected something like this. He opened his mouth to protest, but thought better of it. It didn't matter what he said; Stafford had already made up his mind.

"In fact," Stafford continued, his eyes flicking to Malcolm with a dismissive coldness, "during the entirety of Thorncroft's

visit, you will remain sequestered in your rooms. Do I make myself clear?"

Sequestered. Like a prisoner. Like a child.

Malcolm felt the heat rise to his face, shame and fury battling for dominance. But maybe—just maybe—this would be the extent of his punishment. A chance to regroup, to think of another plan. He swallowed hard and nodded. "Yes, Father."

"Good," Stafford said curtly, turning his attention back to the papers on his desk as if the conversation was already over.

Malcolm exhaled shakily, relief mingling with his humiliation. "I'll go to my room, then," he murmured as he turned toward the door.

"Oh, no," Stafford's voice rang out behind him, brimming with something dark and dangerous. Malcolm froze in place, his hand inches from the door handle. "We're *far* from done, Malcolm."

Malcolm turned back slowly. The glint in his father's eyes made nausea rise in Malcolm's stomach. The *real* punishment was just beginning.

MALCOLM STAGGERED INTO HIS ROOM, THE DOOR CREAKING SHUT behind him with a low groan that mirrored the ache radiating through his ribs. His breath hitched as agonizing pain flared up his side, the result of one too many blows landed with unerring precision.

He leaned against the wall, lifting a hand to wipe at the corner of his mouth. His fingers came away smeared with blood —a damning red against the pale skin of his palm. He stared at it for a moment before dragging his hand across his trousers to rid himself of the evidence. The stain remained, refusing to be ignored.

The room was cloaked in shadows, the heavy drapes drawn tightly across the windows. Even though it was late afternoon, Malcolm had no desire to let in the waning sunlight. The only illumination came from a mage-lamp perched on his bedside table.

His quarters should have been a comfort. Instead, Malcolm felt alien in it, a stranger in the place that was supposed to offer sanctuary. This room, with its carefully curated furnishings and trappings of privilege, felt like a cage. It was a costume he had outgrown. It held no reflection of who he was—or who he wanted to be.

Swallowing, he crossed the room, limping into the wash-room where he normally took such care with his grooming. He gripped the basin, staring at the face in the mirror. Blood streaked his cheekbone, a cut just below the swelling curve of his split lip. His left eye was already darkening, an angry bruise blooming like ink spreading through water. For a moment, the sight sickened him, but then...a small, bitter satisfaction crept in.

The man in the mirror looked nothing like Stafford Wells.

But that thought was no comfort. It was a lie. Malcolm knew it the same way he knew that the blood on his hands would never truly wash away.

He turned the tap on, the freezing rush of water biting into his skin. Picking up the soap, he scrubbed at his hands with almost frantic intensity, growing rougher with each pass. His skin turned raw, reddening under the force, but still, the tinge of blood remained. Swirling with the water, it spiraled down the drain like an accusation.

His hands tremored as he finally turned off the water, droplets clinging to his fingers. He let out a shaky breath, his head bowing forward. The warmth of the room did little to thaw the ice in his chest.

His father's voice echoed in his mind, the words sharpened to a razor's edge: "Everything you have—all the comfort, the privilege, the safety—it exists because of what I've done. Because of what this family has done." Malcolm squeezed his eyes shut, trying to drown out the echo. But it was useless.

Opening his eyes again, he forced himself to look at his reflection, but all he saw was failure. He thought about the Wells legacy—the empire built on suffering and control, on the backs of those his father deemed beneath him. Malcolm knew he was just as much a part of that system, no matter how much he wanted to pretend otherwise.

Blood on his hands was inevitable. It was the price of being a Wells.

He clung to the edge of the sink, gripping it as if it were the only thing keeping him upright. Every part of him ached, not from his father's lesson, but from the hollow certainty that he would never escape this. Never be anything more.

Malcolm's thoughts drifted to Flora. He recalled the challenge in her voice when she spoke back to his father. The way she called him *Mal* with a familiarity that felt strange and friendly all at once. Like the name meant something, like he existed as a person outside of the family name.

He wanted to hold on to that—to her—to the hope she represented. But what was the point? What could he do? She didn't understand what it meant to be a Wells, the iron chains that bound him to the family. She could afford to fight back. Malcolm couldn't. He had no leverage, no allies, no way out.

Renauld's words echoed through his mind: *Not a fighter.*

No, he wasn't. He had never been a fighter. And now, when it mattered most, the truth hurt.

He stared at the man in the mirror. A man who couldn't fight back. A man who couldn't stand up to Stafford Wells. A man who would be nothing more than his father's pawn.

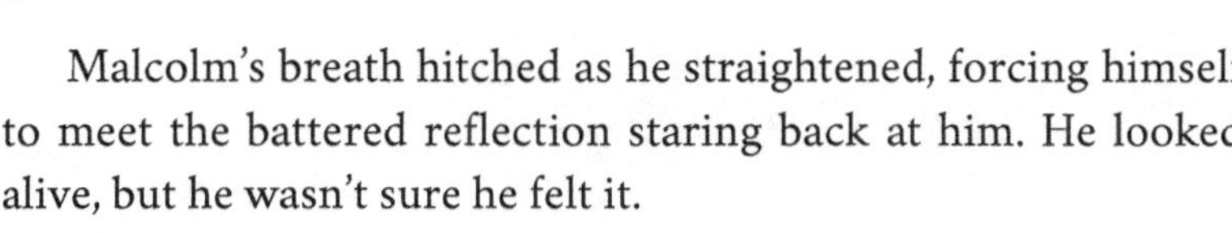

Malcolm's breath hitched as he straightened, forcing himself to meet the battered reflection staring back at him. He looked alive, but he wasn't sure he felt it.

Not anymore.

CHAPTER 10

Flora had never minded small, dark spaces before, but there was something about the Wells dungeon that was stifling, making it hard to breathe. It wasn't just the rats or the damp—it was the knowledge that the walls closing in around her might also close in around the boy upstairs if he didn't grow a spine before it was too late.

The walls were slick to the touch, with moisture trickling through the cracks and pooling in shallow puddles. Flora sat on the cold, wet stone floor, her knees pulled up to her chest. The cell's iron bars filled her vision. She could slip past them easily enough if she wanted—her knocker magic would allow it. It wasn't the lock that kept her in place. It was the game she was playing, the stakes far higher than her own freedom.

"None of these stupid humans ever think to figure out what we're attuned to," she muttered under her breath. Knocker magic wasn't flashy; it wasn't the kind of thing that sparked fear or awe. But if these idiots had any sense, they'd realize it could be devastating in the right—or wrong—hands.

Not that anyone here would bother to ask. No, to them, she was just another thing, a commodity. A creature you threw in a cage when it wasn't working the way you wanted. Flora shook her head, the thought bringing a bitter twist to her lips. Most of the humans who ran this miserable operation didn't even seem to think of her as a person. She might as well have been a tool, or a particularly clever animal.

From down the corridor, the echo of boot steps reached her ears. *Renauld.* Again. Flora stiffened, the muscles in her back tightening as her jaw set. He'd been down here twice already, each time with a fresh round of taunts, circling her metaphorically like a dog with a bone just out of reach. The captain couldn't hurt her, not with a prospective buyer lined up.

Funny how the knowledge that my life is worth coin to line the Wells coffers counts as a comforting thought. Flora sighed.

She could still hear Renauld's voice, slimy with smugness. "You're tough. I'll give you that," he'd said earlier, twirling the key to her cell on a thin iron chain. His dark eyes glinted as he looked her over. Not like a person, but like something on display. "But tough only gets you so far. Especially when the hunter already has you in his sights."

Flora's lip curled. "Hunter? Sounds dramatic, even for you. Is this where you tell me Thorncroft's actually a bad poet?"

Renauld grinned, his teeth flashing wolfishly. "Ah, but you don't know the half of it, do you?" He stepped closer, his voice dipping to a conspiratorial murmur. "Thorncroft doesn't just collect things—he hunts them. Creatures like you, with all your…uniqueness. You're not human enough to belong, and not beast enough to terrify. But rare enough to *thrill* him."

Flora didn't flinch, though her stomach churned. "Sounds like he's compensating for something."

Renauld chuckled darkly. "Oh, I think you'll find his skill speaks for itself. Thorncroft doesn't hunt for sport. He hunts for control. For the pleasure of seeing something wild brought to its knees." His fingers tightened around the key, his eyes narrowing. "And when he's done, he doesn't hang his trophies in

a dusty old hall. No, he likes them alive. Beautiful. Just tame enough to be amusing."

"Let me guess—he stuffs guys like you in jars when he gets bored?" Flora rolled her eyes.

Renauld's grin faltered. "Mock all you want. It won't save you. Thorncroft's already chosen you for his collection. And once he gets his hands on you…well, I suppose you had a good run."

The memory of his words made her growl in frustration. It didn't have to end like this. The truth was, she'd miscalculated. Not entirely—her plan had been solid, but there were too many variables beyond her control. Her knocker magic could only carry her so far, and she had known from the start that the rest of it depended on Malcolm. And that, perhaps, had been her biggest gamble.

That, and assuming the captain's bedwarmer would keep her pretty mouth shut.

The boy—and Malcolm was very much a boy, despite the suit he wore and the airs he put on—had shown promise. Seeds of rebellion, fragile as a snowflake, but there. If only he'd allow them to grow. But his whole life had been built on following rules he didn't write, in playing a game designed so that people like her would lose, no matter the cost.

And here she was, caged.

Still, Flora had seen something in him. Even back at the gala, she'd noticed it. Beneath the pretty facade, behind the careful words and the mask of privilege, there was something else. Something raw and yearning. It wasn't enough—not yet—but it was *there*. And despite herself, she had believed it could be coaxed into something stronger.

He wasn't like his father. That much she knew. Malcolm had a *heart*. But hearts were fragile things, easily blackened or broken. And if Malcolm didn't act soon, Flora feared that hesi-

tation and apathy would shape his heart into the very thing he despised most.

Flora let out an aggravated groan, her head thumping back against the damp, moss-slick wall behind her. She hated feeling like this—trapped, powerless. The anger coursing through her veins was the only thing keeping her in check. If she harnessed it properly, it would fuel her forward momentum.

But anger wasn't enough, was it? Not alone.

She exhaled a gusty breath, pushing the thought away. She couldn't afford to wallow. The sound of footsteps broke into her thoughts. She scrambled to her feet, moving closer to the bars with cautious curiosity. Two guards came into view, their heavy boots scuffing against the floor, escorting a group of prisoners. Flora's heart stuttered as she recognized one of the hunched figures trailing behind them.

"Uncle Jasper," she whispered, her breath catching in her throat.

She forced herself to step back, feigning disinterest, as the guards unlocked the cell beside hers and shoved the prisoners inside. She didn't miss the cruel smirks they exchanged or the way one of them nudged Jasper none-too-gently in the ribs before slamming the door shut. The guards left without a word.

Flora waited until the guards were long gone before approaching the bars, her hands curling around them. The iron felt cool against her palms, but a latent prickle lingered beneath the surface—salt-iron worked into the metal, its presence designed to keep magic users in check. Flora was unbothered by it. "Uncle Jasper!"

Jasper stirred at the sound, lifting his head with a dazed expression. His dark blue hair, nearly black in the wan light, clung to his damp forehead. His pale eyes blinked slowly, adjusting to the shadows of the dungeon. He looked as though he'd been dragged through the depths of a coal mine and left to crawl back on his own.

"Flora…" His voice was rough, raspy, like the scrape of stone on stone. But there was warmth there, too, a familiarity that tugged at her heart. "Little flower."

Her lips twitched at the childhood nickname, a ghost of a smile. Almost. But the tremor in his voice made her brows knit together. "What did they do to you?"

Jasper waved a hand, as if to dismiss her concern, though he was sluggish. "The guards thought it would be amusing to leave me outside for an hour," he said with a dry chuckle that held no humor. "Bright winter sun. No clouds. You know how it is."

Flora bit back a furious growl. He would recover, though the overstimulation of his sensitive eyes would take him a while to work through. "Bastards," she muttered. "I'm sorry."

He shook his head. "Not your fault," he murmured, rubbing at his temples. "But Flora…why are you here? You and I both know you could slip past these bars without breaking a sweat."

"I'm not leaving anyone I care about behind," she shot back, her tone fierce. "I'm not abandoning you. Or anyone else."

Jasper sighed, a deep, weary sound. He shifted closer to the bars, his hands resting just shy of the salt-iron that bound him. "A place like this…" He trailed off, glancing over his shoulder at the others in his cell. A small Knossan child huddled in a corner, horns trembling as he sobbed quietly. Beside him, a lupine Theilian crouched protectively, her arm wrapped around the child's small frame.

"You're not bound as we are," Jasper said, gesturing to the iron bars. "Your magic… You could move freely. Escape."

"I don't care," Flora whispered, shaking her head so that her pink hair fell into her eyes. She shoved it away. "I'm not leaving you."

Jasper's expression grew tender. "Flora, you've always had a big heart," he said gently. "But hearts get crushed in places like this. You need to think about—"

"I *am* thinking!" she snapped, cutting him off. Then she

winced, apologetic. "Sorry. But I'm thinking about *you*, Uncle Jasper. About the others in here. I won't let them keep you."

Jasper studied her for a moment, his pale eyes searching hers. "You've got something in the works," he guessed quietly. "Don't you?"

She hesitated before nodding. "Yeah. I've got a man on the inside."

His brow furrowed. "Who?"

Flora took a deep breath. "The son of the bastard who owns this place."

Jasper's lips twitched into a wry smile, his skepticism flaring. "I don't know if I'd put faith in one of them, Flora," he said. "They're born into this world. They don't see people like us as anything but tools. You're only setting yourself up to be hurt."

Her throat tightened at his words, recalling the savage strike Malcolm had suffered from his father. All because he'd stood up for her. "I'm not the only one who's going to get hurt," she whispered. "Not if I don't do something."

Flora waited until the hour was late, though in the dungeon, it was nearly impossible to tell the time. The dim orange glow of the lanterns lining the corridor never changed, casting the same haunting shadows hour after hour. She could only judge by the guards delivering their evening meals—cold bowls of gruel that did little to satisfy or warm. After two patrols passed her area of the dungeon, Flora decided it was time to act.

In the cell next to hers, Uncle Jasper and the others were asleep. Their slumber wasn't peaceful; it was broken by fits and restless movements, as though they were caught in dreams just as cruel as their waking reality. Flora sat cross-legged on the floor, watching them for a moment. Exhaustion clung to her,

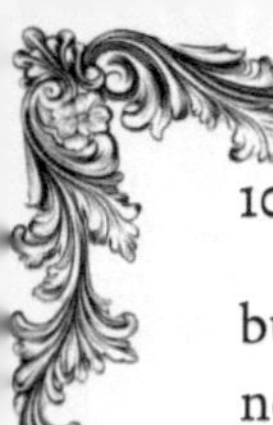

but she'd always been able to get by on minimal sleep. Right now, her purpose outweighed any physical discomfort. She had a mission.

She ran her tongue across dry lips and closed her eyes, unfurling her magical senses like a fisherman casting a net. The process was second nature by now, an extension of herself, as easy as breathing. She reached out, locating every node of the rare metal she was attuned to. The metal that, if these haughty elite found out, would make her worth her veritable weight in gold.

She sensed it in several places across the estate, built into its foundations. Flora frowned, trying to suss out the one she needed. Usually, knockers only called on this ability in the wilds, but Flora had used it extensively on the Wells estate. The knowledge that her excursions would infuriate both Renauld and Stafford Wells cheered her as she decided on her target: a fragment in the servants' quarters.

Focusing on it, she used her magic to *hop*, vanishing from her cell to appear in the quiet quarters.

The servants were sound asleep, their shallow breathing and faint snores serving as background noise. The air here smelled faintly of sweat and soap—better than the dungeon, but still far from pleasant. She wasn't concerned with the servants. They wouldn't wake easily, accustomed to long, grueling hours. Her focus was on her next destination.

Flora didn't know the exact location of Malcolm's quarters, but she was an excellent snoop. The manor was a labyrinth of opulence and excess, but her knack for observation had already marked out where the family likely resided. It didn't take long before she found the right hall, the doors grander and spaced farther apart. She grinned at the absurdity of it all. Even their doors screamed wealth.

She pushed open the one she knew was his. The hinges creaked softly, and the light from the hallway spilled inside

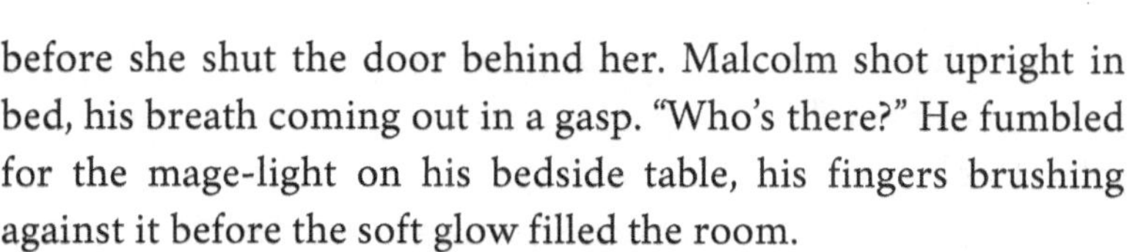

before she shut the door behind her. Malcolm shot upright in bed, his breath coming out in a gasp. "Who's there?" He fumbled for the mage-light on his bedside table, his fingers brushing against it before the soft glow filled the room.

"Just your friendly neighborhood half-knocker," Flora quipped. As her eyes adjusted to the light, she winced. *Schist*, Malcolm looked terrible. His face was mottled with bruises, one eye puffy and dark, his split lip swollen. His movements were stiff as he swung his legs over the side of the bed, wincing.

He stared at her, his expression shifting between disbelief and something almost haunted. "You should go," he said, his voice quieter now but no less strained.

Flora's eyes flashed with annoyance. "People keep telling me that," she grumbled. "But I'm not leaving anyone behind. Not even you." Malcolm's eyes narrowed, and for a moment, she caught a flicker of surprise. It was quickly swallowed by resignation as he shook his head.

"You're not thinking clearly," he said, his tone bereft of hope. "We don't stand a chance against my father. He's bested us at every turn. We can't fight that."

She clenched her fists, wanting to shake sense into him, but knew based on his condition, it was the wrong tactic. His face spoke volumes—the pain, the defeat, the high cost of being Stafford's son. "That monster didn't even get a Healer for you, did he?" she asked quietly.

"Sometimes he does," Malcolm admitted, his voice barely audible. "Not that it makes any of this better. But this…he wants me to *remember* this."

Flora's mouth went dry. "He wants to break you."

"I think I've always been broken." Malcolm's lips curled into a pained, bitter smile.

"Nah." Flora shook her head. Maybe she and the rich boy weren't as different as she had first thought. "You're just the puzzle piece that doesn't fit this particular puzzle."

Malcolm let out a dry snort, which quickly turned into a grimace of pain. "Well, my father is determined to hammer me into place."

She grinned, her confidence unwavering despite the dire circumstances. "While your father is busy putting together a puzzle, let's change the game."

Malcolm's brow furrowed as he gave her a bemused look. "What do you mean?"

"It's time for chess," she said, her grin morphing into something fierce.

Malcolm shook his head, shoulders sagging. "This isn't a game, Flora. We've lost."

"No." Flora stalked closer, her frown deepening. Gods, this was bad. Malcolm's face wasn't the only thing that had been bruised. He looked like someone who had been hollowed out from the inside, his spirit crushed by his father's cruelty. His spine hunched, and his gaze dropped to the floor, as if afraid that meeting her eyes would break him further.

"Look at me," she whispered.

He hesitated, swallowing hard before his gaze finally lifted to hers. Malcolm's eyes were weary, red-rimmed, and filled with an anguish that made her heart hurt. "I appreciate you coming to me, but—"

"Stop talking." Flora's words cut through his protest like a blade. She hadn't meant to sound so snippy, but the edge in her voice startled him into silence, his mouth snapping shut. She exhaled, wincing. "Sorry. Let me finish."

Malcolm nodded, the apple of his throat bobbing as he swallowed again.

"Mal, you've got what, two and a half feet on my height? Not even having human blood made me much bigger than a standard knocker like my uncle." She raised a hand to show the height of her uncle for emphasis, the corners of her lips twitching with the faintest hint of a smile despite the gravity of

the moment. "He's about this tall. I've got a few inches on him, maybe. The point is, I'm small. Always have been. But I've never let that stop me." She sighed, hoping her words would reach him. "I find ways around it. I adapt. Because you know what happens to the ones who don't adapt?"

Malcolm's gaze dropped again, his shoulders tensing. "They die."

"Yeah." Flora nodded, her voice softening as she crouched, trying to pull his focus back to her. "And look, for this, it's hopefully metaphorical. But I've never let my size—or what I am, or who I am—stop me. And you can't let it stop you, either."

His lips pressed into a thin line, and his eyes flicked back to hers. There was something new in his gaze now—not hope, but maybe the faintest spark of curiosity. "Why did you come to me tonight?"

Flora blinked, caught off guard by the question. She hadn't expected him to ask. "Because that monster you call a father hurt you," she said plainly. "And that…it's not right. You don't deserve that. I wanted to make sure you were okay."

Malcolm was quiet, his brow furrowing as he mulled over her words. After a long pause, he spoke again. "No one's ever done that before for me, besides my sister." He hesitated, then added, "Checked on me like this, I mean."

Flora's eyebrows rose slightly. *Sister.* He'd mentioned a sister in passing previously, but Flora had been too distracted by other matters to ask. And now probably wasn't the best time, either. But what happened to this mysterious Wells daughter? *And why haven't I seen her on the estate?* Malcolm probably didn't feel up to an interrogation from Flora, though. "Yeah, well," she said, trying to lighten the mood. "I can't leave you here to be abused again. You're far too pretty for that."

Malcolm let out a low chuckle. The effort clearly pained him, his expression tightening as he gritted his teeth against it.

"So, chess, you say?" he rasped, glancing up at her with a ghost of amusement in his eyes.

He was interested! Hope flared in Flora's chest. "I've got some ideas," she said, tamping down her excitement. "But it's up to you to tell me if they'll work or not. Because I thought maybe this time, we leave the plan up to me."

Malcolm nodded slowly, but his expression shifted into something almost cunning. There was a glint of calculated resolve in his gaze that hadn't been there before. "I want to hear your plan," he said, his voice steadier now. "But I have a suggestion I want you to keep in mind."

Flora tilted her head slightly, pleased to see him ready to engage. She gestured for him to continue. "Sure. What are you thinking?"

His gaze held hers, determination suddenly bright in his eyes. "We don't just change the game. We change the players."

CHAPTER 11

Malcolm exhaled a long, shaky breath as he leaned over the heavy wooden desk in his study. The wintry sunlight filtering through the window painted the room in dull shades of amber and grey. His ribs protested with every shift, each twinge a reminder of his father's "lesson." The ache ran deep, a cold, persistent burn that flared whenever he breathed too deeply. Still, he refused to let the pain slow him down.

The study smelled of ink and paper, with a faint undercurrent of furniture polish. Father might have sequestered him to his rooms, but he hadn't forbidden him from handling the lesser aspects of the family business. That loophole, Malcolm realized with grim satisfaction, was now the heart of Flora's plan.

Her gutsy, brilliant, possibly impossible plan. Malcolm still marveled at it. Even enhanced with his suggestion to "change the players," it was precarious at best. But desperation polished resolve into a formidable tool, and Malcolm was learning to handle his with skill.

Letters lay on his desk in neat stacks, the ink still drying on some. They bore the mark of a new breed of collaboration:

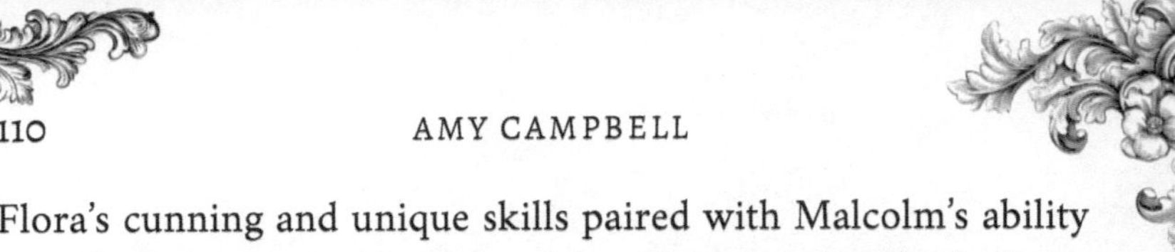

Flora's cunning and unique skills paired with Malcolm's ability to navigate the intricate web of elite egos and double-dealings. Each letter was a seed of doubt, a whisper of suspicion, sent to the right ears in Stafford Wells' sphere of influence. Starting with Silas Thorncroft.

Their plans unfurled long after the manor settled into uneasy quiet. When the halls were empty, and the servants and guards had retreated to their quarters, Flora slipped away into the night like smoke on the wind.

Malcolm had provided the intelligence—maps, letters, and details about Thorncroft's estate culled from dusty journals of long-dead relatives who had reveled in the Thorncroft family's hospitality. Flora had taken it from there, vanishing into the darkness armed with weaponized documents and an audacity Malcolm could only envy. She had infiltrated Thorncroft's grounds, leaving incriminating evidence in carefully chosen locations where it was guaranteed to be discovered by staff or visitors.

"Trust me," she had said before disappearing that first night. "He'll believe what he sees. The stuff you dug up? It's solid."

Malcolm rubbed his forehead, his fingers pressing against the dull ache blooming there. The numbers on the ledger in front of him blurred together, but he forced himself to keep going. He couldn't stop. Not when they were so close to disrupting the delicate balance his father relied upon to maintain his stranglehold over so many lives.

There was an ember burning inside him now. It stirred to life whenever he thought about Flora, her words cutting through his self-pity and despair like a blade. She had been concerned about him—*truly* concerned—and that concern had shaken something loose in him.

For the first time in years, Malcolm could imagine the possibility of a different life. A different version of himself.

It wasn't just Flora's words that stayed with him. It was the

way she had looked at him, as if she could see past the bruises, past the layers of his father's indoctrination, to the person buried deep within. She had seen the Fraction of Something More that Malcolm had nearly let himself forget existed—the part of him that craved freedom as fiercely as Flora did.

Straightening his posture with a wince, Malcolm focused on the ledgers spread across his desk. Each page was a minefield of names, dates, transactions—a sickening map of power, control, and corruption. The Wells family network was vast, its influence woven into every aspect of their business. At first glance, it seemed impenetrable. But Malcolm knew better. He had been raised in its shadows, had been trained to wield its tools. He knew where to look for the weaknesses, the loose threads waiting to be pulled.

By nightfall, his desk was a chaotic sea of open ledgers, scattered papers, and hastily scrawled notes. Crimson ink marked the pages, encircling key names and linking events that might otherwise have seemed unrelated. *It seems I have more letters to pen.* Malcolm was halfway through another ledger, scanning for connections, when a soft pop snapped him out of his thoughts.

Flora's arrival was as sudden and quiet as always. Malcolm had given up trying to understand how she moved around so efficiently. "Knocker magic," she'd said with a breezy shrug the first time he'd asked, making it clear she wouldn't say more. He still didn't find that explanation *remotely* satisfying.

"That's unnerving. Are you aware of that?" Malcolm asked, setting down his pen and leaning back in his chair, smiling. The expression tugged at his still-healing face, but at this point it felt like a gesture of resistance, so he embraced it.

She laughed, the sound bright and ringing. Flora winced mid-laugh, quickly clamping her mouth shut as if realizing she'd been too loud. "You'll get used to it, Mal," she said, the teasing lilt of her voice sending an unexpected warmth through him.

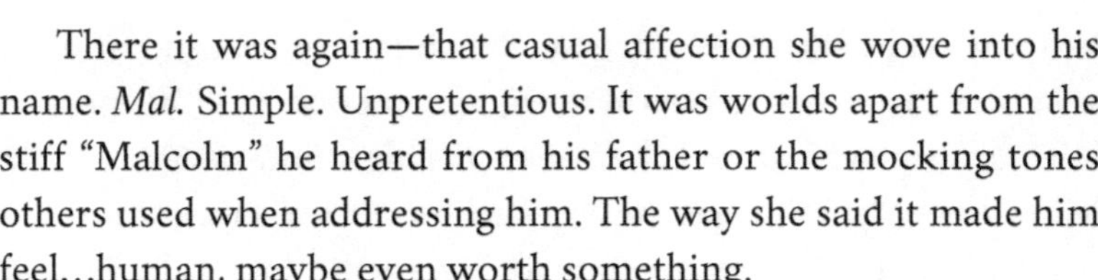

There it was again—that casual affection she wove into his name. *Mal.* Simple. Unpretentious. It was worlds apart from the stiff "Malcolm" he heard from his father or the mocking tones others used when addressing him. The way she said it made him feel…human, maybe even worth something.

Before he could dwell on the thought, Flora held up a small velvet box, her grin triumphant. "I got the thing you wanted. And gods, man, this was a *lot* of coin, even for you!"

He chuckled, though the sight of the box had his pulse quickening. He forced himself to appear composed, folding his hands on the desk. "That was every last bit of my Fortune of Majority," he said, his tone light.

Her brows shot up, intrigued. "Fortune of Majority? Sounds fancy. What's that?"

"It's a Gannish custom," he explained, leaning back in his chair as if they were discussing something mundane. "Though it's mostly an elite tradition. When a child reaches adulthood, they're gifted a hundred golden eagles to spend as they please."

Flora cocked her head, her expression somewhere between curiosity and mild disdain. "That's not chump change. And you're buying jewelry? At a time like this?"

"A *strategic* purchase," he said, his grin widening. "Everything we're doing requires a certain…flair for the theatrical." He held out his hand expectantly, and Flora rolled her eyes before dropping the box into his palm.

Malcolm carefully opened the box, revealing the ring nestled inside. His breath hitched. The cabochon-cut ruby glimmered in the light, its deep red hue radiating an almost hypnotic warmth. To most, the piece would seem gaudy, ostentatious even. But Malcolm knew better. The value wasn't in its appearance but in what it could *do*.

Wetting his lips, he slipped the ring onto his finger. For a moment, nothing happened. Then, warmth flared across his

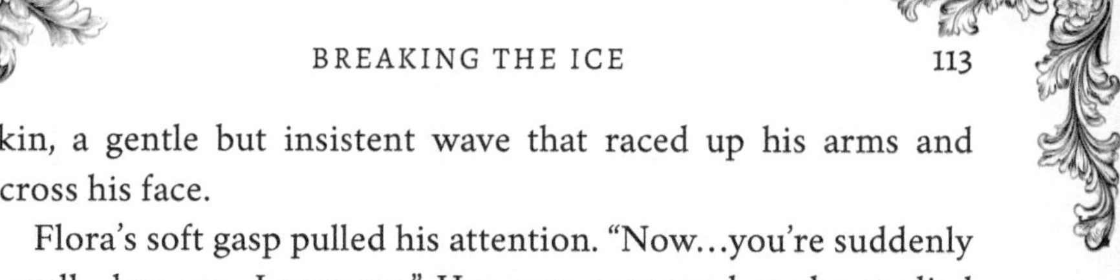

skin, a gentle but insistent wave that raced up his arms and across his face.

Flora's soft gasp pulled his attention. "Now…you're suddenly —well—less *you*, I suppose." Her eyes narrowed as she studied him.

Malcolm pulled open a drawer and retrieved a small hand mirror. What he saw made him pause. His usual dark hair was now a rich blond, and his jawline had softened, making him look more approachable. Intense green eyes stared back at him, bright and unfamiliar, free of the bruises and wear that Stafford's *lessons* had left behind.

"Well?" he asked, arching a brow as he turned sideways toward Flora. "Do I look ridiculous?"

She looked him up and down, as if he were a sculpture. Or perhaps a horse at auction. "Nah. You're still a pretty boy. Blond could grow on me."

"Fantastic. I'll take that to heart." Malcolm chuckled, the sound almost giddy. For a moment, he let himself revel in the possibilities the ring offered. It was like trying on a new life—a life free of his father's shadow, of the family name that clung to him like chains.

"You still sound like *you*, though," Flora pointed out, breaking the moment with her practical observation.

He nodded, reluctantly pulling the ring from his finger. The warmth dissipated, replaced by his old self. "True. But we'll just have to hope that one arrogant elite sounds much like another, hmm?"

"Oh yeah," Flora said, nodding far too quickly. "You all do sound pretty much the same."

"I'll pretend that doesn't hurt my feelings," Malcolm replied dryly, setting the ring back into its box. He closed the lid with a soft snap, a renewed determination settling over him. "But what matters is we've changed the players."

A week later, Flora wiped her damp forehead with the back of her hand, steam swirling around her like the world's most humid blanket. The bathhouse walls seemed to close in, and the cloying lavender scent did nothing to hide an undercurrent of fear that turned her stomach. She kept her head down, hair sticking to her temples, deliberately avoiding the guards' gazes lingering too long by the door. She fought the urge to lash out, knowing she couldn't trust herself not to snap if she locked eyes with them, keeping quiet instead.

She focused on the task at hand, scrubbing her arms with fragrant soap. Around her, the other captives attacked their skin with matching urgency, as if vigorous washing could scour away the reality of their situation along with the grime. Then the command of a guard tore through the low murmur of water, snapping everyone to attention instantly.

"Be quick about it," he snarled, his voice ricocheting off the tiles. "You're not here to be pampered."

Pampered? Yeah, who do I complain to about the lack of hospitality? Flora bit the inside of her cheek, forcing herself to swallow the retort. She had learned to temper her responses, pushing

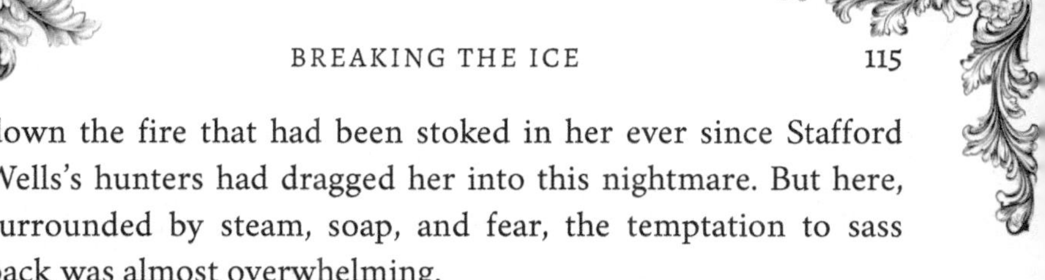

down the fire that had been stoked in her ever since Stafford Wells's hunters had dragged her into this nightmare. But here, surrounded by steam, soap, and fear, the temptation to sass back was almost overwhelming.

Not now. Not yet. Keep calm. Keep quiet. Malcolm would keep to the plan. He had to.

Jasper's voice echoed in her memory from that morning, whispering through the bars of their cells. "Don't let him see your fear, little flower."

"I'm not scared for *me*," she'd hissed back, clutching the bars in a death grip. She hadn't lied: fear had always been reserved for the ones she couldn't protect. Now, that knowledge weighed heavily on her as she glanced at her uncle in the bathhouse, the trembling Knossan child, and the lupine Theilian woman whose uncanny quiet belied a soul-deep despair in her eyes.

Flora growled to herself. She'd do everything in her power to keep them safe. Too bad the guards had confiscated her knife. Its serrated edge might have made a compelling argument—especially if planted squarely between Stafford's cold, dead eyes.

"Move." A guard shoved her shoulder, jolting her out of her thoughts.

The shove was more of a suggestion than a demand, but Flora still bristled, her jaw tightening as she kept her hands to herself. She stepped barefoot out of the bathhouse, leaving damp footprints on the floor. The thin shift they'd given her clung to her skin, offering no real warmth against the chill. She barely had time to wring out her hair before a guard pressed a new bundle into her arms—a sleek but scratchy scrap of lace and thin fabric, plainly designed more to reveal than protect—offering absolutely no warmth at all.

Her lip curled, but she tugged it on anyway. The high collar chafed her neck, and the clinging black dress left her feeling exposed despite its coverage. A costume, nothing more.

Merchandise. That's what she was to them. That's what they all were.

The others shuffled along behind her in silence. Jasper walked with the heavy slowness of someone resigned to his fate, while the Knossan child clung to the Theilian woman's side, his small hand gripping her sleeve. No one spoke. No one needed to.

As Flora shuffled into the atrium with the others, her gaze was drawn—against her better judgment—to the towering glass panels lining the far wall. Beyond them, the estate's frost-covered grounds stretched out like a postcard no one asked for. A carriage rolled up the long gravel drive, the horses' breath visible in the cold air. She winced. That had to be Silas Thorncroft.

As much as she wanted to study her potential enemy, Flora needed to get the lay of the land. The moment she stepped into the atrium, the cold hit her like a slap, harsh enough to make her shiver. The space sprawled outward, caught between a ballroom and a greenhouse, as if its designer had thrown money at both ideas and called it a day.

Marble floors gleamed beneath the glow of crystal lanterns, their light scattering across the room in fractured patterns. Greenery draped from the railings, vines curling around columns in a way that was meant to look natural but only really underscored the illusion: wealth dressed up as wilderness, fooling no one.

At the center, a fountain commanded attention, rising high with tiered marble bowls overflowing into a wide basin. Water streamed from the mouths of carved cherubs, their faces frozen in perpetual bliss. Gilded ivy wrapped around the structure, gleaming beneath the lanterns. The steady trickle might have been calming if the cold mist it threw into the air didn't make it feel like standing too close to an open ice box.

And there was Stafford Wells, planted beside the fountain as

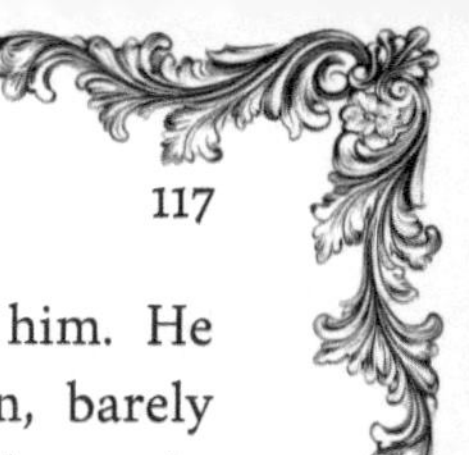

though it had been designed specifically to frame him. He tugged at his silver cravat with an air of irritation, barely glancing at the poor servant scrambling to meet his demands. His coat—deep green with silver trim—blended seamlessly with the garish decor. *Naturally.* Flora swallowed a bitter laugh.

Did he reupholster the furniture to coordinate with his outfit? Wow. The scene practically reeked of carefully curated holiday cheer—bowls of gilded pinecones lined the tables, and the towering evergreen near the fountain gleamed with glass ornaments, as delicate and cold as the man standing beside it. All for show.

The patter of hurried footsteps pulled her attention toward the northern doorway, where a servant slipped in with a silver tray bearing a decanter of mulled wine and glasses trimmed with sugared rims. Otherwise, the atrium was stiflingly orderly, a tableau of power and oppression laid bare. It was very…*transactional.*

The double doors groaned open, drawing everyone's attention as a butler entered first. Stafford turned, his expression shifting to one of nonchalance as he sank into one of the high-backed chairs by the fountain. With one hand resting on the armrest and the other smoothing the fabric of his coat, he waited, poised like a lion.

His guest had arrived.

Silas Thorncroft stalked in. Flora could almost feel the plants shrinking back from the man's sinister aura. Even the fountain seemed to quiet as he passed.

"Ah, Master Thorncroft," Stafford drawled, turning with a flourish that practically oozed faux charm. His arms spread wide like a seasoned showman about to unveil his greatest trick. Or, Flora decided, a carnival showman hoping to part a fool from their money. "It's an honor to have you here. I trust your journey was pleasant?"

Silas Thorncroft studied Stafford as if he saw right through

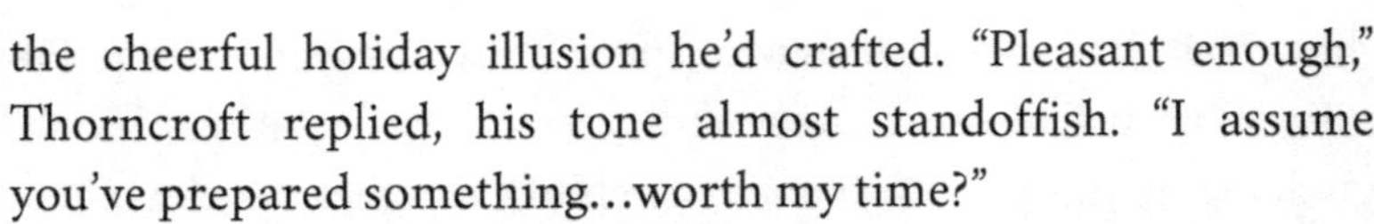

the cheerful holiday illusion he'd crafted. "Pleasant enough," Thorncroft replied, his tone almost standoffish. "I assume you've prepared something…worth my time?"

Flora dropped her gaze, knowing it was best if she didn't stare. She didn't dare lift her head, not even when her skin prickled with the man's approach. *Stay quiet. Stay invisible.* That was the game. Just for a little while longer.

Stafford wasted no time launching into his pitch, his voice smooth and unhurried as he extolled the so-called virtues of his *merchandise.* He exaggerated characteristics, spoke of strength, of unique traits, as if her uncle were livestock and the Knossan child was a decorative trinket.

Flora was very proud that she didn't lunge at him in a murderous rampage at that point. *Hooray for self-control.*

Thorncroft stood by the fountain, his posture as rigid as the carved cherubs spitting water. With his dark suit and calculating stare, he looked less like a guest and more like a man deciding whether to buy the whole estate just so he could burn it down later.

As Stafford droned on about "unique lineage" and "once-in-a-lifetime acquisitions," Flora's gaze snagged on movement beyond the glass panels of the atrium's far wall. She squinted, straining to see through the light frost clinging to the panes. A figure moved along the drive leading to the estate—just one, and too far away to make out details. Her heart gave a small, traitorous lurch. *Is it him?*

The elder Wells continued, undeterred, his voice rising and falling in a rhythm that was almost hypnotic. She tried not to look again, but it was impossible. The figure was closer now, and—gods—was that a blond head catching the pale winter sunlight? She risked another glance. No mistaking it this time. That coat, those boots…Malcolm, in his enchanted disguise, strode toward the atrium as though he owned it. Her breath hitched. He wasn't just acting now; he had *become* the role. If he

could keep it up, maybe they had a chance. And gods help them all.

Flora averted her gaze again. Wouldn't do to clue anyone in to his impending arrival.

A servant cleared his throat, drawing Stafford's attention and his ire. He turned to glare at the man. "Why do you dare interrupt me?"

The servant looked as if he'd rather be covered in honey while facing a bear just waking from hibernation. "Sir, there's… someone to see you. He says it's an urgent business matter."

Stafford scowled, his arms crossing tightly over his chest. "I'm busy," he snapped. "Tell whoever it is to wait."

The servant hesitated, his gaze shifting to Thorncroft before returning to Stafford. "He insisted, sir. And…he's already here."

Stafford's scowl deepened, annoyance rolling off him in waves. But before he could respond, the doors swung open fully, revealing the interloper. Tall, poised, and impeccably dressed in a deep-blue waistcoat, the newcomer moved with the kind of confidence that bordered on vanity. Blond hair framed a shrewd but charming face, and his green gaze swept across the room, missing nothing.

Flora clamped down on the ridiculous grin blooming on her face. *Of course, he shows up looking like he just won the lottery of swagger.* But beneath the snark, a kernel of hope broke through fertile soil. Malcolm was here.

"Oh, is this a bad time?" he asked, his voice rich and self-assured. There was no hint of apology in his tone, only a polished veneer of politeness.

Stafford's expression darkened like a brewing storm, his jaw tightening visibly as he gestured toward the intruder. "Who in the name of the gods dares interrupt me during a business meeting?"

The man didn't flinch. If anything, his smile widened, a picture of disarming charm as he strode further into the atrium.

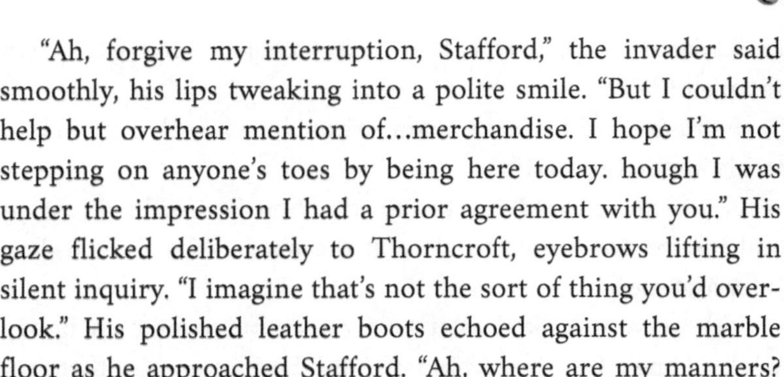

"Ah, forgive my interruption, Stafford," the invader said smoothly, his lips tweaking into a polite smile. "But I couldn't help but overhear mention of...merchandise. I hope I'm not stepping on anyone's toes by being here today. hough I was under the impression I had a prior agreement with you." His gaze flicked deliberately to Thorncroft, eyebrows lifting in silent inquiry. "I imagine that's not the sort of thing you'd overlook." His polished leather boots echoed against the marble floor as he approached Stafford. "Ah, where are my manners? Apologies, I thought you remembered. Jefferson Cole, of course." He dipped his head with an air of casual politeness.

Flora almost laughed with relief—and it was good she didn't, or that would have given everything away. Stafford probably would've imploded if he realized he was being outmaneuvered by his own son. Now *that* would've been a show.

Malcolm's voice was unchanged, but everything else about him felt like a brand-new creation: no more fearful heir, no more skittish nerves. He stood tall, unrelenting, as Stafford stared, dumbfounded. This version looked ready to sell Stafford a bridge and expect a thank-you in return.

Jefferson's brows lifted ever so slightly, as if taking pity on the elder Wells. "You *do* remember, don't you?"

Stafford blinked, his temper momentarily derailed by sheer astonishment. His mouth opened, then closed, like a man trying to bite down on a word before it could betray him. Flora watched with mild amusement. If his brain was a train, it had just derailed spectacularly and taken the entire station with it.

"Jefferson Cole," he repeated, testing the name as if its syllables might reveal some hidden meaning. Flora could practically see the wheels turning behind his beady eyes, analyzing, cross-referencing his mental ledger of contacts and rivals. But no match emerged. "Who invited you to my estate, Mr. Cole?"

Jefferson didn't flinch at the question. Instead, he clasped his hands neatly behind his back, radiating self-assurance that

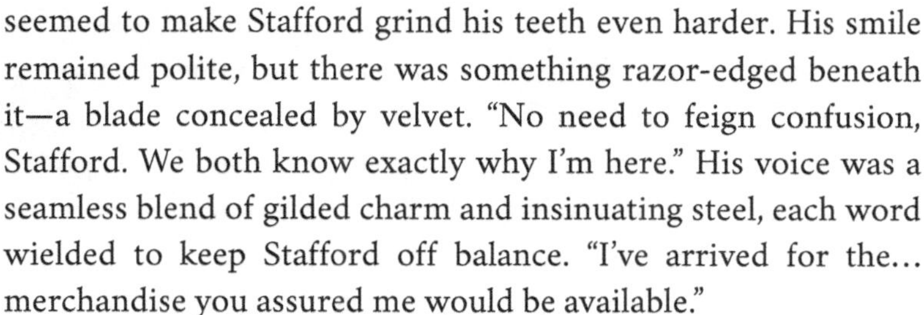

seemed to make Stafford grind his teeth even harder. His smile remained polite, but there was something razor-edged beneath it—a blade concealed by velvet. "No need to feign confusion, Stafford. We both know exactly why I'm here." His voice was a seamless blend of gilded charm and insinuating steel, each word wielded to keep Stafford off balance. "I've arrived for the… merchandise you assured me would be available."

Flora's shoulders stiffened involuntarily. She didn't dare lift her head, but she could feel the shift in the air. It rippled across the room like a stone tossed into still water, the other captives going rigid as they tried to suppress any visible reaction. For her part, Flora kept her breathing calm, though her mind raced. This was the crux of the plan, and Malcolm—Jefferson—was playing his part flawlessly.

Across the chamber, Stafford's confusion gave way to something darker. Anger simmered beneath his carefully controlled facade, the corners of his mouth twitching in a barely restrained snarl. His nostrils flared. "I assured you no such thing," Stafford growled. "I don't even know you."

Jefferson canted his head, his smile deepening as though Stafford's protest was only a tiresome joke. He waved a hand through the air, the gesture dismissive, like he was swatting away a gnat. "Oh, come now," Jefferson said lightly. "Let's not play games, my good man. One of your associates left me very specific instructions—your invitation included."

He leaned forward ever so slightly, just enough to close the distance between himself and Stafford without it being overtly threatening. "Surely a man of your standing wouldn't want word spreading that you failed to honor an agreement."

Jefferson delivered the line smoothly, almost idly, but Flora caught it for what it was—a dagger slipped between the ribs. Stafford Wells was a man used to control, used to power, and now, for the first time in years—decades, perhaps—someone had slipped out of his grip.

"I do *not* know what you're insinuating," Stafford hissed. He rose from his chair. "But there's no invitation, no associate—no sale to you, or anyone else!"

Flora caught Thorncroft shifting where he stood. The gilded buttons on his suit glinted in a shaft of afternoon sunlight as he dipped a hand into the inner pocket of his jacket.

Here we go.

Silas Thorncroft thrust a crisp, folded paper toward Stafford with a movement so threatening it might as well have been a pistol. "Then how do you explain this?" His voice carried the low rumble of thunder before a storm, clipped with irritation and laced with accusation. Apparently, Thorncroft wasn't a fan of Stafford's holiday theatrics, either.

Flora hid a smile, but satisfaction warmed her. She knew exactly which letter Thorncroft had presented—because she had delivered it to him herself. Covertly, of course. It had been Malcolm who uncovered the sordid details buried deep in the ledgers.

Malcolm. His name whispered in her mind as her gaze flicked briefly to the side, catching Jefferson watching the exchange. He looked almost bored, leaning slightly to one side, his fingers idly tracing the hem of his coat as though this were little more than theater for his amusement. But Flora knew better. Beneath the mask he wore, he was just as pleased by the turn of events as she was. Jefferson caught her eye and winked. She almost rolled hers in return, but settled for a sly grin instead.

The man who winked at her now was so different from the one she had first encountered—the hesitant, bruised heir buried beneath his family's name. That Malcolm had flinched in his father's shadow, unsure of his own strength. But this version had broken free from that fear, shedding it like a skin. It wasn't just the ring's magic that had changed him. It was the choices he had made, the risks he had taken, and the quiet work that had brought Stafford's lies into the light. He had transformed, not

just into a new persona, but into someone who could stand in this moment and fight back.

Flora hid a smile at the thought. It was during those long nights, pouring over ledger after ledger, that Malcolm had begun to truly see the shape of the Wells empire. The arrogance that had kept Stafford secure for decades—the same arrogance that had dismissed Malcolm as a pawn—had also created the cracks Malcolm now exploited. Stafford's system, he told Flora, was like a spiderweb: intricate, sprawling, and devastatingly fragile in the right places.

Stafford and his forbearers had played their buyers like puppets, promising captives to multiple elites, lying about their whereabouts, spinning elaborate excuses to mask their double dealings. Names were changed, ages falsified, descriptions altered just enough that no buyer suspected they'd been played. It was a dangerous system. One that relied on arrogance, trust, and the Wells name being untouchable.

But Stafford's hubris had left cracks. And Malcolm had been the one to spot them.

This is how the mighty fall. Flora had told herself that as she planted the seeds of distrust. Letters were delivered, ledgers were copied, and every detail Malcolm uncovered had been weaponized.

Now, Thorncroft stood holding the knife Malcolm and Flora had forged, and Stafford was the fool left bleeding.

"How did you receive this information?" Stafford's tone had shifted, quieter now, his rage like a beast trying to claw its way out. The paper crumpled in his fist.

Flora kept her head down, but inside, she smiled. *All thanks to the half-breed and the son you called an idiot.* The thought thrilled her. She wanted so badly to revel in this small victory, but she couldn't risk tipping her hand.

Thorncroft's lip curled. He didn't answer Stafford's question directly. Instead, he tilted his head, his dark gaze narrowing. "All

of this," Thorncroft said, his voice as smooth as glass, "is *damning*, Stafford. Especially the information copied from the Wells ledgers."

Stafford froze, the red blotches creeping up his neck now meeting the flush of his face. The fountain gurgled loudly, as though mocking him. "The *Wells ledgers?*" His words came out like a growl, his voice shaking with incredulous anger. "How in Perdition do you have access to *those?*"

"Oh, do you mean these?" Jefferson spoke for the first time since the confrontation began, his tone cutting cleanly through the tableau.

He slid a hand into his coat pocket with the flair of a performer delivering the final act. When he withdrew the paper, the subtle rustle was almost theatrical. With the flick of a wrist, he unfolded it, revealing rows of names, dates, and sums. The Wells ledgers, carefully copied.

Stafford's gaze darted to the page, his face slackening for just a moment before twisting into something venomous. The cracks in his composure were no longer cracks—they were fissures splitting wide open. "*Where did you get those?*"

His smile never wavered, but the fire in Jefferson's green eyes revealed a resolve that couldn't be ignored. "That's hardly the question you should be asking, is it?" His voice was dangerous in its ease. Flora was so damn proud of him. "I would be *far* more concerned about why such...oversights exist in the first place. Oversights that paint you in a *rather* unflattering light."

Satisfaction rippled through Flora, though she didn't let it show. Jefferson's words needled at Stafford while Thorncroft reevaluated everything he thought he knew.

Thorncroft's gaze shifted back to Stafford, lingering just a little too long, the unspoken accusation clear in the cold arch of his brow.

Stafford sucked in a breath, his face darkening. "This—this is absurd. My ledgers have never left this estate!"

"Perhaps not, but the information did," Jefferson said softly, almost sounding apologetic. Almost, but not quite. He tucked the papers back into his coat, removing them from the stage, as though to remind Stafford of how little control he now had. "Perhaps someone hasn't been *quite* as loyal to you as you thought."

Stafford looked like a man teetering on the edge of a precipice, his foundation crumbling beneath him brick by brick. "You have no proof of—"

"Proof?" Jefferson interjected. He shrugged, his smile thin but cutting. "Oh, I think we'll find *plenty* before this is over."

Flora kept her eyes fixed on the floor, fighting the grin tugging at her lips. *You're not untouchable, Stafford. Not anymore.*

"*Malcolm,*" Stafford whispered, the name like a curse spat from his mouth. His face darkened, his fury barely restrained behind a mask of brittle composure. He looked ready to storm from the room, but Thorncroft's presence forced his hand. To leave now would be to lose face, and Stafford Wells could not allow that. Not in front of his peers.

"I'm waiting for an answer, Stafford." Thorncroft's tone was laced with iron, his hawk-like eyes fixed on the elder Wells without a hint of mercy. "How do you explain the contents of the letter? The ledgers that correspond with the accusations?"

Stafford's lips twisted into a snarl. "Ledgers can be *falsified,*" he snapped, the words defensive, like a cornered animal baring its teeth.

Jefferson, however, nodded in mock agreement, the picture of thoughtful composure. He clasped his gloved hands loosely in front of him, oozing confidence and disdain. "They certainly *can.*" His tone was so calm it could have been mistaken for sympathy. "The falsification works both ways, though, doesn't it?"

Flora, her gaze firmly downcast, bit the inside of her cheek to keep from grinning. *Oh, he's good.* The subtlety with which Jefferson continued to drip poison into Thorncroft's ear was masterful. The tension in the room shifted yet again, growing taut as Thorncroft turned to Jefferson with a speculative look.

"I've heard enough," Thorncroft announced abruptly, straightening to his full height. "This ridiculous farce is over. I won't let your petty vanity and lies tarnish my name—or worse, risk my fortune." Flora could almost see the invisible coin slipping through Stafford's fingers with each word.

Thorncroft spun and strode toward the exit, the heels of his boots striking the marble like a war drum. As he passed the stunned servant stationed at the door, he snatched his coat from the poor man's trembling hands without slowing his pace.

The door slammed behind him. Silence followed. A single sound—*clack, clack, clack*—broke the stillness as the Knossan child's hooves tapped nervously against the tile. Flora flicked her gaze toward the noise, then forced herself to look away, her face a careful mask of indifference.

Stafford inhaled, the sound scraping against the quiet as he straightened his shoulders. He seemed to be rallying, though the flush of red creeping up his neck betrayed the depths of his fury. His chest heaved as he forced calm over himself like ill-fitting armor. Then his gaze snapped back to Jefferson, more threatening than a drawn blade.

"What's your game?" Stafford's voice was venomous, the words sliding through gritted teeth. "What do you want?"

Jefferson sighed, as though Stafford's reaction was the most tedious thing in the world. He shook his head slowly. "*Want?*" Jefferson echoed, his tone layered with just enough condescension to needle the elder Wells further. "I *want* you to realize what a precarious position you've found yourself in."

"You think you can walk in here and make demands?"

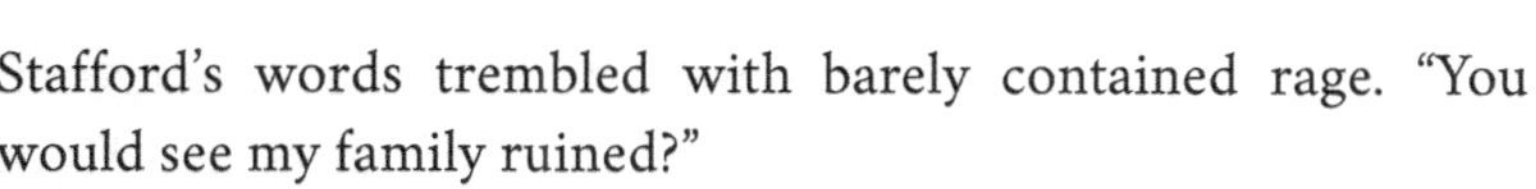

Stafford's words trembled with barely contained rage. "You would see my family ruined?"

Oh, we sure would. Flora smiled to herself.

Jefferson canted his head, his lips slipping into a rueful smile. "That was never my goal," he said, a faint note of bitterness ghosting through his voice. "But yes, I *do* think I can walk in and make such demands, considering the evidence I have on hand."

Stafford's expression twisted, a grotesque mix of frustration, outrage, and mounting desperation. Somehow, his veneer of civility held. Barely. "Fine," he bit out after a beat, his voice a low growl. "You've made your point. How much?"

Jefferson's brows lifted, feigned surprise mellowing his demeanor. "How *much?*"

"Let's make this simple," Stafford snapped, the words tumbling out as though dragged from his throat. "You want to keep quiet? Fine. But you'll name your price." He advanced a step. "You know how this works among people like us."

Flora's head lifted just a fraction, her heartbeat quickening. *Schist.* Would Malcolm take the bait? Stafford's trap was obvious, but his tone—an attempt to rope Jefferson into their shared depravity—was insidious. Could Malcolm navigate this tightrope without falling?

"You misunderstand, Mr. Wells." Jefferson's reply was deceptively casual, but the sly grin tugging at his mouth hinted at the blow he was about to deliver. "The price isn't for *my* silence. It's for *your* freedom to continue operating in polite society."

Stafford blinked, caught off guard by the twist. He froze, his expression unreadable save for the angry twitch of his jaw.

Jefferson allowed the pause to marinate, savoring the elder Wells' unraveling composure. Then he delivered the final blow. "Five hundred golden eagles should suffice. Along with the immediate release of all your...merchandise, of course."

Stafford's face flushed a dangerous shade of purple, his

shoulders rising with indignation as he took yet another step forward. He was perilously close to Jefferson now—and Flora didn't like it one bit. She remembered only too well the brutal hit Stafford had dealt Malcolm.

But right now, he *wasn't* Malcolm—and that made all the difference in the world.

"The money is a simple thing. Consider it done." Stafford's voice crackled like brittle ice. "But your other demand? It'll be a cold day in Perdition before I allow *that.*"

Flora tensed, her stomach souring. *There it is.* Of course, Stafford Wells wouldn't fold. A man like him would never see the lives of his captives as anything other than a commodity to protect.

Jefferson, however, didn't flinch. He shrugged, as though Stafford's refusal was nothing more than a minor inconvenience. "In that case," Jefferson said, his voice light, "make it a thousand golden eagles."

Stafford looked as though he might combust, his body quaking with impotent rage. "This group isn't worth even a *quarter* of that!"

Jefferson shrugged one shoulder and waved a dismissive hand. "Your merchandise isn't my concern. Your questionable *practices*, however, *are.* And I *will* be compensated for my silence."

Stafford's hands clenched, his teeth grinding audibly. "*Fine.*"

Without missing a beat, Jefferson extended his gloved hand. "Pleasure doing business with you."

Flora watched as Stafford hesitated, staring at Jefferson's hand as though it might bite him. Finally, with a jerk of his arm, he gripped it in a single, grudging shake.

And that was how Jefferson Cole gained the beginnings of his fortune.

While Flora appreciated both the artistry and audacity of the performance, it still didn't get her or the others out of this

scrape. Not yet. Malcolm had been adamant in their planning—he *refused* to buy their freedom. "If I do that," he'd argued, "then I'm no better than my father. Even with the best intentions."

She hadn't agreed with him then. She wasn't sure she agreed with him now. But as Jefferson Cole swept from the atrium richer than when he'd entered, Flora couldn't help but wonder if Malcolm had double-dealt *her*, too.

CHAPTER 13

Malcolm studied his reflection in the mirror, slipping the cabochon ring off his finger. He watched, intent, as the magic unraveled. The borrowed features melted away like snow in spring. What remained was unmistakably him: nearly black hair brushing against a pallid complexion, bruises spreading like violets across his cheekbone and jaw, the striking angles of his inheritance evident in his face. His father's marks. His legacy of pain.

The early afternoon light filtering through the window fractured into weak shards, drawing long shadows across the polished floor. Outside, rare snowflakes danced past the glass. Malcolm stared at his reflection for another beat, then returned the cabochon ring to its velvet box. He sighed, dropping the box into the pocket of his coat rather than hiding it in his bedside drawer.

Jefferson Cole had served his purpose. *Now it's time for Malcolm Wells to find his courage.*

His ribs ached as he inhaled. But the pain felt different now. Instead of weighing him down, it fueled something fierce and determined in his chest. He thought of Flora, of her uncle, of the

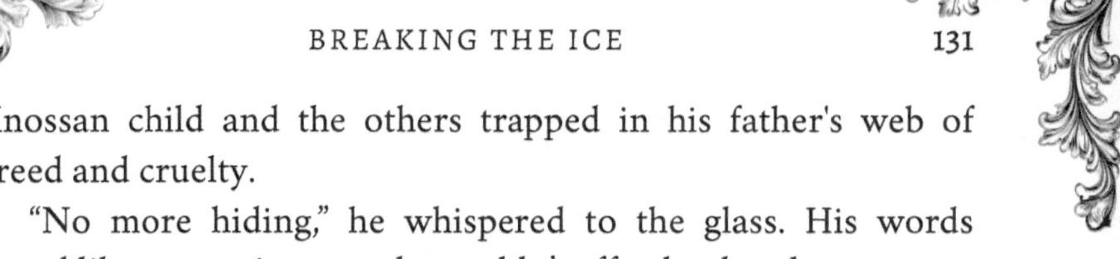

Knossan child and the others trapped in his father's web of greed and cruelty.

"No more hiding," he whispered to the glass. His words tasted like a promise—one he couldn't afford to break.

Time was working against him. Stafford had made the connections, realizing Malcolm was the one disseminating the information. If Stafford caught him here, the fallout would be swift and merciless—not just for him, but for Flora, her uncle, and anyone else Stafford deemed disloyal.

The thought sent a chill through him. *Move.*

Malcolm grabbed his coat from where it hung on the back of his chair, shrugging it on with a grimace. The thick wool settled across his shoulders like iron plating, heavy but necessary. His muscles complained as he straightened and pulled the coat tight, but he refused to let the pain slow him. The door clicked softly behind him as he stepped into the hall, his boots muffled against the thick carpets.

Endless and silent, the manor's corridors stretched ahead, like the throat of some great beast waiting to swallow him whole. Gilded wallpaper and ornate moldings loomed on either side. Wealth paid for in blood. *No more.*

Servants scattered at his approach, pressing themselves against walls or ducking into doorways. Malcolm didn't look at them, though he felt their stares. They must have sensed the change in him—the cowering heir replaced by something harder, more determined. Or perhaps they simply feared being caught in whatever storm was brewing between father and son.

The glass doors leading to the garden appeared ahead, filtering the weak sunlight. Beyond them lay his destination. The secret entrance to the dungeons waited there, hidden among the hedges and overgrown stonework. He reached for the handle, his fingers curling around the cold brass—

A glimpse of distant movement stopped him cold.

Through the glass, the winter garden unfolded in a palette of

white and grey, frost clinging to the tangled hedges like spider silk. At the center of it all, Captain Renauld strode across the gravel path. But it wasn't Renauld alone that made Malcolm's blood freeze in his veins.

Behind him marched a line of captives. Flora was among them.

Even in the bitter cold, she carried herself with her chin raised and shoulders square. Her pink hair still caught what little light broke through the clouds.

A muscle in Malcolm's jaw twitched as anger and fear surged through him, twisting his insides into knots. The fear wasn't for himself, though. It was for *them*. Flora and the others. His grip on the door handle tightened until his knuckles blanched white.

Steeling himself, Malcolm shoved through the doors, the hinges creaking in protest. The sudden rush of cold air bit at his bruised face, but he barely noticed.

Renauld turned, his hawkish gaze locking onto Malcolm immediately. "Master Wells. Shouldn't you be in your quarters?"

"I needed some fresh air," Malcolm replied evenly, though the tightness in his throat betrayed his effort to sound calm. He stepped forward, his boots crunching against the gravel. The frost-bitten air stung his bruised skin, but he met Renauld's gaze without so much as a flinch. "Is that a problem?"

Renauld's gloved hand hovered at the pistol on his hip, his thumb grazing the hammer. He didn't draw it—he didn't need to. Instead, his lips quirked into a condescending sneer. "Of course not, Master Wells. You're free to roam as you please. But your *father*—" He drew out the word *father* like it was a leash wrapped tightly around Malcolm's neck. "—made it clear you were not to interfere."

Malcolm smiled, shaking his head. "That's unfortunate. You see, I'm here to do just that." He held Renauld's gaze as he advanced a step. "To interfere."

Renauld's eyes narrowed, the pistol still untouched but no

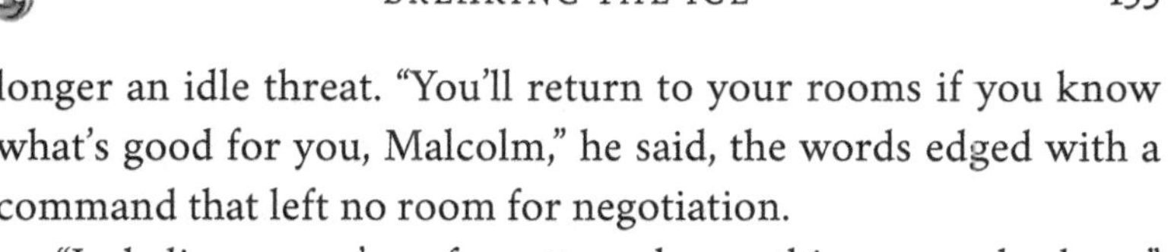

longer an idle threat. "You'll return to your rooms if you know what's good for you, Malcolm," he said, the words edged with a command that left no room for negotiation.

"I believe you've forgotten how things work here." Malcolm's voice cut through the frigid air like a scalpel. "You don't command me. It's the other way around. And now I command you to release—"

"*Malcolm!*"

The roar thundered across the garden, loud enough to silence the wind itself. It was a voice that rattled windows and shook the earth beneath his feet. Stafford Wells appeared like a storm rolling in, his heavy coat billowing behind him and his face contorted with fury. He was the incarnation of wrath, his boots slamming against the frost-touched ground like a prelude to war.

"Bastard. *Traitor.*" Each syllable cracked like a whip.

Malcolm turned slowly, his breath catching. His entire body ached with the memory of their last encounter, but somehow, his voice stayed steady. "Father." The single word was almost civil, almost an invitation. "We need to talk."

Stafford's cutting laugh split the air. "*Talk?*" He growled the word as though it were beneath him, his eyes glinting with danger. "After what you've done?" He advanced a step, a storm on the horizon. "You dare to stand there and speak to *me* of conversation when you've betrayed your own blood?"

"I betrayed nothing," Malcolm replied. He forced himself to stand straighter, to meet the storm head-on, though every nerve in his body screamed to cower. He pulled on the remembered victory of Jefferson Cole to bolster his courage. Malcolm could stand up to his father as *himself*. He had to. "I simply showed the truth where you dealt in lies."

The first blow came so fast that Malcolm didn't even see it coming. Stafford's ring-heavy knuckles struck his jaw with a sickening crack, whipping his head to the side. A flash of white

exploded across his vision, and the taste of copper flooded his mouth. His knees buckled, and he stumbled, catching himself against the wrought-iron garden fence as his ribs shrieked in protest.

Flora's voice rang through the garden, shrill with alarm, but it was distant through the ringing in his ears. Malcolm didn't know if she called his name or simply shouted in anger. He blinked hard, fighting to steady himself, to shake off the haze as Stafford's voice slammed into him again like a hammer.

"Truth?" Stafford stalked after him, invading Malcolm's space even as he struggled to remain upright. "You know nothing of truth, boy. You're weak. Pathetic. And now you're a traitor to your own name." Malcolm had no time to react before Stafford grabbed his collar in an iron grip and yanked him upright, their faces mere inches apart. His father's breath was hot and foul against his cheek. "I should kill you where you stand."

The threat hung in the air for a heartbeat. Something flashed in Malcolm's peripheral vision—a blur of movement. Then Stafford stiffened, his eyes widening as a flash of steel appeared at his throat.

Flora.

She clung to Stafford's back and shoulders like an enraged squirrel, one of the guard's own knives gleaming in her hand. Her arm was steady, the blade biting just enough into Stafford's skin to make her point. Her violet eyes blazed with fury.

"What I lack in height," she snarled, "I make up in rage. And I promise, if you so much as look cross-eyed at him, you'll be eating through a new hole." A single bead of blood welled up where the knife pressed, and Stafford's grip on Malcolm's collar faltered, if only for a moment.

"Get off me, you *filthy creature!*" The fear in Stafford's voice made the command lack its usual punch.

Captain Renauld's pistol was out now, his gaze locked on Flora. "Drop the knife," Renauld ordered.

"Don't," Malcolm said suddenly, though he rubbed his freshly bruised face with one hand. The authority in his tone surprised even himself, and for a fleeting moment, Renauld hesitated. "I wouldn't. You might be fast, Captain, but she's faster. And she has nothing left to lose." Then Malcolm added, "Besides, you risk shooting your employer."

"That's a risk I'm willing to take," Flora chimed in, leaving Malcolm to wonder if her stony skin would protect her from a bullet.

Renauld's jaw tensed, but he didn't pull the trigger.

Stafford's face darkened, his fury boiling over as he glared at his son. "You would let this—this *animal*—threaten me? Your own *father?*"

Malcolm met his father's gaze, unflinching. For the first time, he saw Stafford Wells not as a self-appointed king to be feared, but as a man—flawed, bitter, and small. "No," Malcolm said quietly. "I would let this *person* defend herself and the people she cares about against a monster."

Stafford's eyes narrowed to slits, but he said nothing. The hatred in his glare spoke volumes, however,

"Let them go, Father," Malcolm continued, his resolve unshakable. "All of them. End this now."

"Or what?" Stafford sneered, though the effect was somewhat diminished by the gleaming knife at his throat.

"Or I take everything." Malcolm's voice hardened. His gaze didn't waver as he leaned closer, the frigid wind teasing strands of his dark hair across his bruised face. "The ledgers, the letters, the evidence of your corruption—it all goes public. The Wells name you're so proud of becomes worthless overnight."

Stafford's nostrils flared. He didn't release Malcolm's collar, despite the threat.

Malcolm continued, his voice dropping to a dangerous

whisper. "And we both know what happens to men like you when they lose their power. The vultures you dine with will tear you apart the moment you fall."

Stafford's face contorted with rage, but beneath it, Malcolm saw something he'd never witnessed before—uncertainty. His father's grip loosened as his gaze darted between Malcolm and the knife at his throat, calculating odds and outcomes like the businessman he was.

"You wouldn't dare," Stafford growled, but the words landed weakly. He released Malcolm's collar, shoving him back as though the very contact burned. "You'd destroy yourself along with me."

"Perhaps." Malcolm straightened his collar, ignoring the throb of pain in his face where his father had struck him. "But I've learned something recently, Father. Some things are worth more than the Wells name."

A snowflake drifted between them, landing on Stafford's sleeve before melting away. The garden had grown still, as if nature itself held its breath. Even Renauld and his guards seemed frozen, watching the tableau unfold. Their breath misted in the freezing air, though none dared to speak.

Stafford finally broke the silence, his words forced through clenched teeth. "What do you *want?*"

Malcolm's answer came without hesitation. "Their freedom." He gestured to Flora and the others. "All of them. And your word—witnessed by everyone here—that you'll *never* pursue them."

Flora pressed the blade a fraction harder against Stafford's throat. "He's being generous," she added, her voice carrying a dangerous edge. "I'd have demanded your blood. *Lots* of it."

Stafford's jaw worked silently, veins bulging at his temple as his face flushed an alarming shade of red. His pride warred visibly with his calculations, his glare darting between Malcolm and Flora's knife as though weighing his options. When he

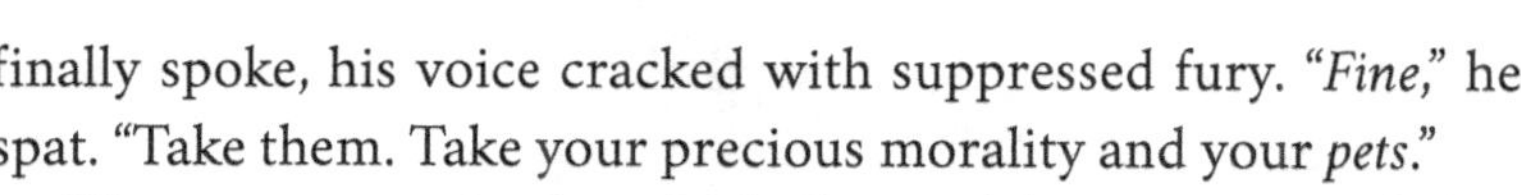

finally spoke, his voice cracked with suppressed fury. "*Fine,*" he spat. "Take them. Take your precious morality and your *pets.*"

His gaze swung back to Malcolm, and for a moment, father and son locked eyes—one blazing with hatred, the other with chilling calm. "But know this," Stafford continued, venom dripping from every syllable, "you are no longer my son. You are *nothing* to me."

"Not a day passed that I felt like your son," Malcolm replied quietly, feeling as though a door was closing behind him. "Trust me, I've lost nothing."

Stafford's eyes narrowed, as if he were preparing to fire another volley. "Oh, you've lost more than you know. What of your precious engagement to Cinna Smithstone? You think she'll take you *now,* disgraced and without a coin to your name?" He laughed, the sound mocking. "That alliance was your *one* redeeming contribution to this family, and now you've ruined even that."

Malcolm's mouth twitched, but it wasn't quite a smile. "*Cinna?*" he said, his tone dry and dismissive. "She's as heartless as the rest of you. I'd sooner spend a lifetime alone than chained to another gilded monster."

A flash of fury sparked in Stafford's eyes, but Malcolm didn't give him the satisfaction of letting his father have another word. Instead, he turned to Flora. "I believe you can release him now."

Flora made a disappointed sound. "I could carve your name on his neck if you want. You know, like a memento for your dear old father."

Stafford stood frozen, alarmed. Renauld cursed. Malcolm's brows flew up. "Thank you for the offer, but that won't be necessary."

"Hear that?" Flora hissed to Stafford. "You got off easy. *Remember that.*" Then she hopped down, moving to Malcolm's side. The other captives quickly gathered behind them, hope and disbelief warring on their faces. The Knossan child clutched

the Theilian woman's furry hand, his eyes wide with uncertainty.

"Captain," Stafford barked, fingers brushing his neck where Flora's blade had pressed. "Let them pass."

Renauld hesitated. Malcolm stared him down. "You heard him. Don't make this worse for yourself."

A muscle jumped in Renauld's jaw, but after a beat, he stepped aside, his anger etched into every line of his face. The other guards exchanged uneasy glances before following suit, creating a narrow path toward the manor's gates.

"Who's a good boy? You are!" Flora said brightly to Renauld, waving at him. The captain's face darkened further, but he didn't move.

Malcolm turned to the captives—his gaze resting on the knocker who was surely Flora's uncle, the Theilian woman, and the wide-eyed Knossan child clutching her hand—and gestured for them to move forward. "Go," he whispered. "We'll cover you."

Malcolm waited, watching them, before pausing and glancing back at Stafford one last time. His father stood where they'd left him, rubbing at the red mark on his neck, his glare simmering with unspoken rage.

"Happy Midwinter, Father," Malcolm called, infusing his voice with cheer.

The low, frustrated growl that escaped Stafford's throat brought Malcolm a grim satisfaction. He turned, setting off after the others, the wind tugging at the hem of his coat as if urging him onward.

Flora fell into step beside him, still holding the knife. "He'll come after you," she murmured, her voice barely audible over the crunch of frozen gravel beneath their boots. "You know that, right?"

"Yes." Malcolm didn't look back, his gaze fixed ahead as the

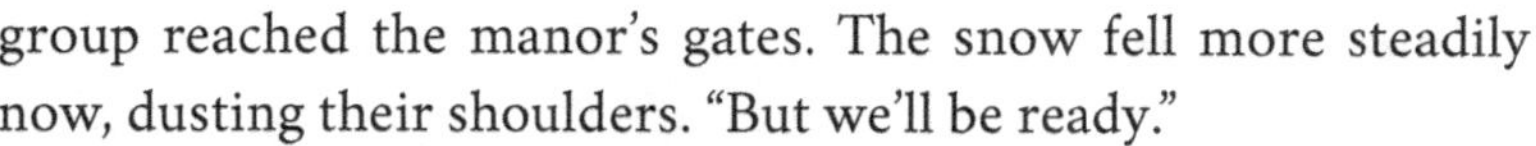

group reached the manor's gates. The snow fell more steadily now, dusting their shoulders. "But we'll be ready."

At the edge of the estate, where the manicured grounds gave way to the wilder world beyond, Malcolm paused. Flora touched his arm lightly and gestured to the older knocker man rubbing his arms in the cold. "Mal, this is Jasper—my uncle. He's the one who taught me most of what I know about sneaking around places like this. The one I wouldn't leave behind."

Jasper managed a thin smile through chattering teeth. "A pleasure to meet you," he said, his voice gruff but warm.

Malcolm offered a smile of his own. "I owe you for teaching her so well."

Jasper snorted, his breath misting in the air. "Let's call it even once we're all far away from here."

Flora cackled as she fell into step with her uncle.

Malcolm turned back to look one last time at the place that had been his home—and his cage. The Wells manor loomed in the distance, its grey stone exterior darker against the muted sky. Its windows stared back at him like hollow, unblinking eyes, watching his departure with silent judgment. A wintry wind blew through the branches above, tugging at his coat like invisible fingers.

He glanced at the others. The small group huddled together for warmth, their breath fogging the frigid air. Not a single one of them wore a coat or anything substantial to shield against the creeping winter chill. The Knossan child shivered against the furred Theilian woman while Jasper rubbed his arms in vain, trying to fend off the bitter cold.

"I'm a fool," he whispered bitterly. "My father only allowed your release because he knew the elements would serve as your punishment."

Flora, standing beside him, gave a quick nudge to his side followed by a mighty eye-roll. "You and your father aren't the only ones playing this game. Everyone, follow me."

Brows raised in curiosity, Malcolm obeyed. The group trudged after Flora as she veered off the beaten path, guiding them away from the open road and into the surrounding woods. Iced-over branches snagged at their sleeves as they moved single file through the overgrown brush. They were cold and weary, but Flora's pace never faltered, and her confidence seemed to offer the group a sliver of hope.

After several minutes, she stopped beside a fallen tree, its massive trunk hollowed out by time and decay. "Here we go." Flora reached into the dark recess of the hollow and began pulling out canvas bags, their weight making a satisfying *thump* as they landed on the frozen earth. She opened one, pulling out a thick blanket. Flora held it up with a broad grin, like a hunter showing off a prize buck, before rifling through the rest of the bags. Blankets, coats, additional clothing, bundles of food—hard, dried rations, but food nonetheless—emerged like treasure.

"What is all this?" Jasper asked, his scratchy voice tinged with disbelief as he crouched beside Flora, inspecting the bounty.

Malcolm stared at the bags, recognition dawning as the pieces fell into place. He recalled the missing supplies from the estate, the inconsistencies in the records that had first drawn his attention, the subtle disappearances of minor items over weeks. "You *beautifully* cunning person," he breathed.

Flora grinned up at him, her expression flashing with mischief. "Been planning this for a while. I've got supplies hidden all around the perimeter. This was just the closest stash." She dusted her hands off on her trousers and tossed a coat to the shivering Knossan child, who clutched it gratefully.

"Brilliant," Malcolm murmured, watching as the group dug into the bags. Jasper pulled a heavy blanket around his shoulders, breathing out a contented sigh. The Theilian woman

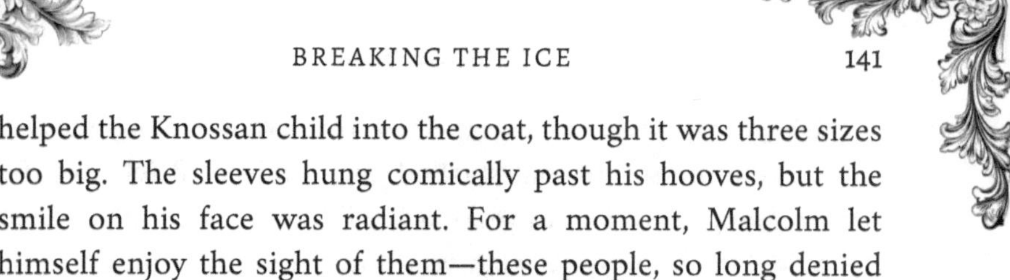

helped the Knossan child into the coat, though it was three sizes too big. The sleeves hung comically past his hooves, but the smile on his face was radiant. For a moment, Malcolm let himself enjoy the sight of them—these people, so long denied even the smallest comforts, finding some measure of relief.

"Happy Midwinter," Flora said, patting the little Knossan on the back.

"Happy Midwinter, indeed," Malcolm murmured, swallowing as he realized the enormity of the gift Flora had given him.

Before long, everyone had bundled up, cozy in the liberated coats and blankets. The supplies were distributed among them and they set off once more.

Malcolm and Flora fell behind, walking in quiet tandem a few paces behind the group. The branches of surrounding trees clattered as the wind picked up, scattering late season leaves across their path.

"Thank you," Malcolm said after a long moment, his voice quiet but sincere. "For what you did back there."

Flora snorted, as if brushing off his gratitude. "Did you forget what I said?" She glanced sidelong at him. "I needed to make sure everyone I care about gets out of that glorified torture chamber. *Including you.*"

The fierceness in her words caught him off guard. Malcolm blinked, struggling to swallow the sudden tightness in his throat. "I wasn't sure," he admitted. "I thought maybe—"

Flora flailed a hand to cut him off, as though swatting away a bothersome insect. "You think I was just saying that to win you over? Oh, *no*, Mal. Haven't you learned by now? I'm as blunt as a hammer to the head." She canted her head, fixing him with a pointed look. "I'll always tell you like it is. Including if I hate your guts." She paused, laughing at the look that crossed his face. "Which I don't, by the way. Your guts are pretty good."

Her words were so unexpected that Malcolm laughed, a rough, genuine sound that startled even himself. It felt like the first *real* laugh he'd had in years, a small burst of warmth against the cold. "Well, I'm quite glad you don't," he said, smiling as he adjusted the canvas bag on his shoulder. It was heavier than he cared to admit, and he could feel it pulling at his still-healing ribs.

Flora rolled her eyes at the sight of his struggle and edged closer, plucking the bag from his grip with a grumble. "Hand it over."

"I can handle it," Malcolm protested. His ribs disagreed.

The half-knocker patted his arm, shouldering the bag as if it weighed nothing at all. "Maybe so, but this is what friends are for, right?"

Friends. Malcolm swiped a hand at his misty eyes. He didn't know if Flora understood the impact of her words, and at the moment, he was feeling *far* too many emotions to discuss any of them properly. Malcolm chose to change the subject, at least for now.

He glanced ahead at the group, now just silhouettes moving through the skeletal trees. "I'm not sure what comes next."

Flora glanced at him, her expression unusually serious. "Well, first things first. We find a place to stay for a while, so we can figure things out. That part might be dicey. I was able to smuggle out items, but not funds. Your father had those locked up tighter than a nun in a brothel."

Malcolm choked back his reaction, schooling his features. *I can see she intends to keep me on my toes.* He rather liked that. "No, it won't be difficult at all."

Flora shot him a questioning look, one brow arched. "What's that supposed to mean?"

Now it was his turn to surprise her. Malcolm grinned. "Our friend Jefferson Cole has recently come into a *considerable* amount of funds," he explained, chuckling. Gods, that was *satis-*

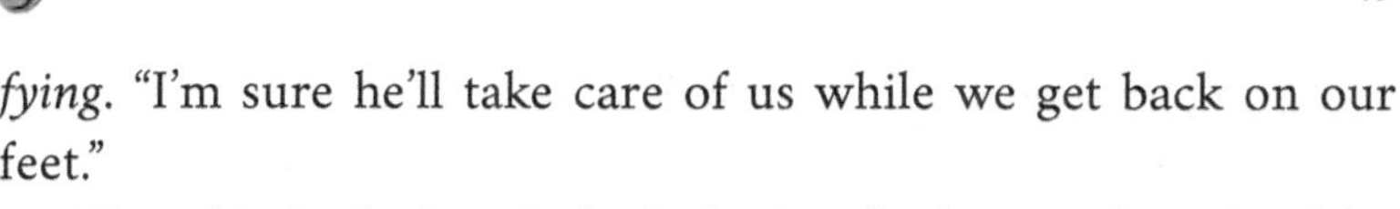

fying. "I'm sure he'll take care of us while we get back on our feet."

Flora blinked, then hefted the bag higher on her shoulder with a snort. "Come on," she said, jerking her chin toward the narrow road ahead. "We can talk as we walk." She fell into step beside him. After a moment, she glanced sideways at him, curiosity dancing in her eyes. "Wait. That part was real?"

"Very real," he confirmed, his voice lighter than it had been in weeks. "Some of those letters I had you send out? They were to a contact I have—a fixer of sorts—someone skilled at creating identities. They set Jefferson Cole up as a *very* real person, complete with a fabricated history, citizenship records, and a bank account sorely in need of funds." He shook his head, still marveling at it himself. "Before I left, I made sure to leave a calling card in my father's study with the necessary information to transfer the funds into the proper account."

Flora let out a low whistle, clearly impressed. "That's slyer than I expected from you, Mal. Nicely done." Her eyes glittered with approval and admiration. "So you're planning to use this Jefferson Cole front whenever we need it? Just a disguise to get us settled somewhere new?"

Malcolm hesitated, his gaze wandering to the snowy canopy above them. A few snowflakes drifted lazily down, swirling like flecks of starlight through the branches overhead. Such an unusual sight for Ganland. It was a shame he couldn't properly enjoy it. He held out a palm to catch a snowflake. "Not just a front, Flora. I think…" He paused, testing the idea in his mind before continuing. "I think I'd like to *be* him. Jefferson Cole."

Flora raised an eyebrow, her expression skeptical but amused. "Okay, but why *Jefferson Cole?* Of all the names you could've picked, you went with *that?* Sounds like a shady horse trader who swears he's got the best mares in Ganland but sells you a swaybacked mule instead."

Malcolm gave her a sideways glance, his lips quirking. "It has

a nice ring to it. Strong. Reliable. The sort of name people trust." He shrugged. "Besides, it's not tied to anything—or anyone—that can be traced back to the Wells family. That's the whole point."

She considered this, her nose wrinkling slightly as though tasting the name again. "Hmm. I guess it works. But…" Her grin turned mischievous. "Can I call you Jeff?"

"Absolutely not," Malcolm replied without missing a beat. It was his turn to wrinkle his nose. *Jeff? Really?*

Flora snorted, her grin widening. "Fair enough." Her teasing faded, though, as her lips pursed. "So Malcolm Wells would be no more?"

Malcolm shook his head. "Not quite. My plans are still in their infancy, but..." He tossed a look over his shoulder toward the manor house now hidden by trees. "If the Wells name caused harm for so many, perhaps I can also use it to right the wrongs. But through proper channels. Perhaps political channels."

Flora let out a dry laugh and shoved her hands into her pockets. "Politicians are just one step away from what your father is, Mal."

"Some," Malcolm agreed with a nod. "But not all. And someone has to try to be better." His gaze grew distant. "I won't pretend I'll be perfect. No one is. But I think…" He swallowed hard, his next words as soft as the snowflakes settling on their shoulders. "I think it might be my best chance to do what's right." He turned to her then, his dark eyes meeting hers. "And, no offense to you, but I think I need to begin with humans first. The mages."

Flora nodded, absorbing the information. "Yeah, makes sense. I know a lot of humans don't see us mystic races as the same."

"Even though you are," Malcolm replied, a smile warming his face as he looked down at her. The honesty in his tone made

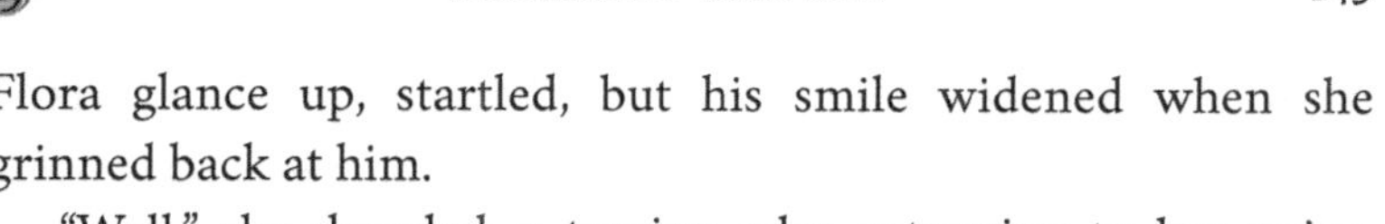

Flora glance up, startled, but his smile widened when she grinned back at him.

"Well," she drawled, a teasing edge returning to her voice, "it's a long road, Mal. Possibly a hard one." She gave him a pointed look. "And it sounds like you'll need allies."

Malcolm took a slow breath, the snow falling more steadily now around them. "That's what I wanted to ask you," he admitted. "Flora, would you help me? As I begin this? I know it'll take time—and I'll make certain to pay you fairly—"

Flora stopped walking and whacked his arm lightly with the back of her hand. "*Stop*," she said with mock exasperation. "Sure, I'll help you. I don't have anything better to do, so I could carve out some time to help you bring down an oppressive system." She slid him a sly look. "And while I'd do it for free—because I do enjoy making some good trouble—a girl's gotta eat. So pay would be nice."

Malcolm laughed again, the sound ringing clear and genuine. It felt like the cold air couldn't reach him anymore, not with her beside him. His heart warmed as he looked at Flora— the small, brave woman who had stood by him, fought for him, and helped him find the courage to forge a new path.

As they stepped further into the unknown, leaving the Wells estate behind, the snow drifted silently around them, coating the world in a thin veil of white. For the first time in his life, Malcolm felt as if his choices and actions *mattered*. The road ahead might be uncertain, winding and full of obstacles, but it was his.

And he wouldn't walk it alone.

Jefferson, Flora, and the other outlaws will return with more adventures!

But if you enjoy watching magically-inclined sad boys make

noble-but-terrible decisions while falling for the last person they should trust—Cedric's here to ruin your night (and possibly your heart). Get ready for *Scales and Steel*!

ALSO BY AMY CAMPBELL

Tales of the Outlaw Mages

Breaker

Effigest

Dreamer

Persuader

Songbinder

Heartseeker

Airship Dragons

Dragon Latitudes

Dragon Meridians

The Gilded Prince

Scales and Steel

Talons and Treason

Novellas

Dawn of the Jade Empress (Airship Dragons)

Breaking the Ice (Tales of the Outlaw Mages)

www.ingramcontent.com/pod-product-compliance
Lightning Source LLC
Chambersburg PA
CBHW021716190726
48289CB00008B/2553